A CASE
FOR
SEXTON
BLAKE

Francis Durbridge

WILLIAMS & WHITING

Cover design by Timo Schroeder

9781915887405

Williams & Whiting (Publishers)
15 Chestnut Grove, Hurstpierpoint,
West Sussex, BN6 9SS

Titles by Francis Durbridge published by Williams & Whiting

1   The Scarf – tv serial
2   Paul Temple and the Curzon Case – radio serial
3   La Boutique – radio serial
4   The Broken Horseshoe – tv serial
5   Three Plays for Radio Volume 1
6   Send for Paul Temple – radio serial
7   A Time of Day – tv serial
8   Death Comes to The Hibiscus – stage play
     The Essential Heart – radio play
     (writing as Nicholas Vane)
9   Send for Paul Temple – stage play
10 The Teckman Biography – tv serial
11 Paul Temple and Steve – radio serial
12 Twenty Minutes From Rome – a teleplay
13 Portrait of Alison – tv serial
14 Paul Temple: Two Plays for Radio Volume 1
15 Three Plays for Radio Volume 2
16 The Other Man – tv serial
17 Paul Temple and the Spencer Affair – radio serial
18 Step In The Dark – film script
19 My Friend Charles – tv serial
20 A Case For Paul Temple – radio serial
21 Murder In The Media – more rediscovered serials and
     stories
22 The Desperate People – tv serial
23 Paul Temple: Two Plays for Television
24 And Anthony Sherwood Laughed – radio series
25 The World of Tim Frazer – tv serial
26 Paul Temple Intervenes – radio serial
27 Passport To Danger! – radio serial
28 Bat Out of Hell – tv serial
29 Send For Paul Temple Again – radio serial
30 Mr Hartington Died Tomorrow – radio serial

Murder At The Weekend – the rediscovered newspaper serials and short stories

Also published by Williams & Whiting:

Francis Durbridge: The Complete Guide
By Melvyn Barnes

For more information about Francis Durbridge please visit:
www.francisdurbridgepresents.com

INTRODUCTION

Francis Durbridge (1912-98) was a prolific writer of sketches, stories and plays for BBC radio from 1933. At first they were mostly light entertainments, including libretti for musical comedies, but a talent for crime fiction became evident in his early radio plays *Murder in the Midlands* (1934) and *Murder in the Embassy* (1937). The *Radio Times* (11 February 1938) mentioned that Durbridge had by then written some one hundred radio pieces, and Charles Hatton commented in *Radio Pictorial* (28 October 1938) that "He is one of the very few people in this country who have succeeded in making a living by writing for the BBC."

Durbridge's defining year on the radio was 1938, when he created the dream team of novelist/detective Paul Temple and his wife Steve. The eight-episode radio serial *Send for Paul Temple* was an immediate success that attracted over 7,000 listeners' requests for more, which led to numerous sequels until 1968. Indeed Paul Temple in the mid-twentieth century became a leading light in the extensive list of popular radio detectives that included Dick Barton (by Edward J. Mason), Philip Odell (by Lester Powell), Dr Morelle (by Ernest Dudley), PC 49 (by Alan Stranks) and Ambrose West (by Philip Levene).

As well as writing the Paul Temple serials, Durbridge contributed to BBC radio for many years with numerous plays and serials under his own name and sometimes as Frank Cromwell, Nicholas Vane or Lewis Middleton Harvey. Then in 1952, while continuing to write for radio, he embarked on a sequence of BBC television serials (not featuring the Temples) that achieved huge viewing figures until 1980. He also wrote nine intriguing stage plays, produced from 1971 in the UK and even earlier in Germany, including *Suddenly at Home, Murder with Love* and *House Guest*.

While much of this information will already be known to Durbridge fans, the fact that he wrote a radio serial featuring the legendary Sexton Blake might come as a surprise. This was *A Case for Sexton Blake*, broadcast from 12 March to 16 April 1940 in six episodes and included in the BBC Home Service programme *Crime Magazine*, produced by William MacLurg and featuring Arthur Young as Blake and Clive Baxter as his assistant Tinker. The contract to write this, given the iconic character and worldwide following of Sexton Blake, was something of an honour – although richly deserved in Durbridge's case, given his standing at that time as the pre-eminent writer of radio serials. *A Case for Sexton Blake* is an atmospheric thriller enhanced by the regular intrusion of the haunting "Song of Death", specially composed by the prolific Eric Spear (1908-66), whose many later works were to include television's *Coronation Street* theme.

The popularity of Sexton Blake has endured since Victorian times. His debut, *The Missing Millionaire*, was written by Harry Blyth (1852-1898) using the pseudonym Hal Meredeth and published in the magazine *The Halfpenny Marvel* on 20 December 1893, after which Blake appeared in many other magazines throughout several decades. His original persona as a rival of Sherlock Holmes (with both living in Baker Street) has been constantly updated by numerous writers, but it is the *Sexton Blake Library* that is best remembered today. This series of magazines on cheap paper ran from 1915 to 1968, and among the army of writers in its later years appeared such well-known names as John Creasey, Jack Trevor Story, Rex Hardinge, Michael Moorcock, Anthony Parsons, John Newton Chance, John Drummond, Desmond Reid, Arthur Maclean, W. Howard Baker and Stephen D. Frances. And in addition, much to the confusion of bibliographers, many *Sexton Blake Library* writers not only used their own names but adopted house pseudonyms to fit into the series by switching styles between classic detection, suspense and espionage.

Sexton Blake and his entourage appeared throughout the twentieth century in every medium – in print, on the radio, on television and in the cinema. Radio manifestations over the years saw him played by George Curzon, Arthur Young, William Franklyn and Simon Jones; on television by Laurence Payne and Jeremy Clyde; and in the cinema by C. Douglas Carlile, Hans Hubert Dietzsch, Douglas Payne, Langhorne Burton, George Curzon, David Farrar and Geoffrey Toone.

But perhaps at this point it is worth putting Durbridge's Sexton Blake radio serial in the context of his early career, given that his first radio credit on 25 July 1933 (*The Three-Cornered Hat*) was a play for children that was far removed from the crime genre in which he was to achieve international renown. He followed this with more children's stories and plays and light-hearted musical shows, but on 3 October 1934 his first serious drama *Promotion* was broadcast. At that stage, within a varied output, his crime fiction credentials began to emerge. *Murder in the Midlands* (1934) and *Murder in the Embassy* (1937) are already mentioned above as significant productions, but the most enduring example of his new trend was his series of career-defining radio serials beginning with *Send for Paul Temple* (1938), *Paul Temple and the Front Page Men* (1938) and *News of Paul Temple* (1939).

Following *A Case for Sexton Blake* in 1940, Durbridge regularly contributed to BBC radio with crime dramas featuring one-off investigators. Stuart Vinden was Anthony Sherwood (1940-41), Carl Bernard was Johnny Cordell (1941), Frances Clare was Amanda Smith (1941-42), Rita Vale was Gail Carlton (1943-44), Henry Oscar was Michael Starr (1944), Kenneth Kent was André d'Arnell (1944) and Bernard Braden was Johnny Washington (1949). And although none of these characters survived into lengthy series, it can be conjectured that Durbridge was leaving his options open and not assuming that Paul Temple would guarantee his permanent reputation.

There is no doubt that Francis Durbridge regarded himself primarily as a playwright, although many of his radio and television serials were novelised and thirty-five books were published from 1938 to 1988 bearing his name. But now the publication of his recently discovered script of *A Case for Sexton Blake* will give today's readers their first opportunity to enjoy this adventure of an iconic sleuth scripted by a twentieth century master of radio mysteries.

Melvyn Barnes
Author of *Francis Durbridge: The Complete Guide* (Williams & Whiting, 2018)

This book reproduces Francis Durbridge's original script together with the list of characters and actors of the BBC programme on the dates mentioned, but the eventual broadcast might have edited Durbridge's script in respect of scenes, dialogue and character names.

A CASE FOR SEXTON BLAKE

A serial in six parts
By FRANCIS DURBRIDGE
Broadcast on BBC Radio
12 March – 16 April 1940
CAST:

Sexton Blake . . . . .Arthur Young
Tinker . . . . Clive Baxter
Tony Carradine . . Ben Wright / John Robinson
Peter Marthioly . . . . .Wilfrid Walter
Joan Dixon . . . . .Jane Grahame
Benito Marthioly ………..…….………John Morley
Angus …………………….……………… Cyril Nash
Inspector MacTaggart …….…..…………Foster Carlin
Siboku ……………..……….…..…………Ewart Scott

EPISODE ONE

MURDER
WEARS A MASK

OPEN TO:

VOICE: (*Deep and rather sombre*) The Castle of Saint Marguerite stands in sombre majesty in the midst of a murmuring lake. About its grey turrets gulls wheel and scream in the winds of the Northumbrian night.

FADE IN noise of seagulls and an approaching storm.

VOICE: Within the castle all is silent. A seven-foot wall of age old granite shuts out the wild wailing of the stormy night.

FADE noises completely.

VOICE: Sleep has indeed laid its silence upon the house of Marthioly.

There is a pause.
FADE IN the sound of a man breathing.
He is obviously a fairly heavy sleeper.
Suddenly, the sound of a door is heard.
There is a slight pause.
The sleeper awakes.
He is obviously terrified and utters a sudden shriek.
He struggles.
It is quite obvious that he is slowly being strangled.
He gives a last desperate cry for mercy.
He is answered by a low deliberate chuckle.
FADE IN of music.

FADE DOWN music completely.

TINKER: You haven't opened the telegram, guv'nor .

BLAKE: (*Pleasantly*) The telegram? Oh yes … the telegram. It can wait, Tinker. It can wait.

TINKER: (*Anxiously*) But – but guv'nor, it might be important!

1

BLAKE: Important? It probably is, Tinker, but then just at the moment so is this omelette. (*Amused*) And never keep an omelette waiting, my boy! Never keep an omelette waiting! (*Eating*) My word, Mrs Bardell seems to have excelled herself!

TINKER: It's all very well you pulling my leg, but this telegram …

BLAKE: (*Laughing*) All right, Tinker! All right!

BLAKE tears open the envelope.

There is a pause.

TINKER: What … what is it?

BLAKE: (*Quietly*) You were right, Tinker. This is important … Desperately important!

TINKER: (*Obviously impressed*) What … What is it?

BLAKE: It's from Tony Carradine.

TINKER: Tony Carradine? You mean … Carradine of The Daily Star?

BLAKE: Yes.

TINKER: (*Anxiously*) Guv'nor … you look worried!

BLAKE: Listen to this, Tinker. (*Reading*) "To Sexton Blake. Please come Saint Marguerite at once stop. The Man in the Iron Mask walks again stop. I need your help. Carradine."

TINKER: (*Puzzled*) The Man in the Iron Mask? What the Dickens does he mean?

BLAKE: Tony's mother is a member of the Marthioly family, and the Marthiolys are the descendants of the original Man in the Iron Mask.

TINKER: (*Bewildered*) The … original … Man in the Iron Mask? You mean to say there was a bloke who went about in an iron mask on his napper …?

2

BLAKE: Yes, a Count Aldo Marthioly. And his only crime was that he looked exactly like King Louis the Fourteenth of France. For that reason he was imprisoned in the island Castle of Saint Marguerite.

TINKER: Blimey!

BLAKE: Aldo's wife, seeking sanctuary from the wrath of Louis, came to England with her children. Charles the Second took pity on her plight and gave the family an old lake bound castle in Northumberland. They called it Saint Marguerite to remind them of the place where the unhappy Count was a prisoner. After the death of his father Aldo's eldest son obtained the Iron Mask and brought it to England.

TINKER: You mean to the castle?

BLAKE: Yes. And according to legend the ghost of poor Aldo followed the mask to its last resting place and still haunts the castle of Saint Marguerite.

TINKER: Still haunts the castle …? Crikey! Why that's exactly what …

BLALE: Exactly what Tony Carradine says … "The Man in the Iron Mask walks again …"

TINKER: (*Staggered*) But blimey, you don't believe in this ghost business, guv'nor?

BLAKE: I don't know, Tinker. I don't know. But I do know that Tony Carradine must have been pretty desperate to have sent me a telegram like this.

TINKER: (*Thoughtfully*) Yes. Yes, that's true enough.

BLAKE: And there's another point, Tinker. The legend of the Man in the Iron Mask might well provide a convenient cloak for the activities of a clever criminal. (*Casually*) Pass me the telephone.

3

A tiny pause.

BLAKE: Thanks.

BLAKE dials a number.

TINKER: But suppose there is a criminal, guv'nor – what's he after?

BLAKE: The Marthioly family is a fairly wealthy one, Tinker. And where there is wealth there is also the motive for crime.

TINKER: (*Quietly*) Yes. Yes, I suppose that's true. (*Suddenly*) Who are you ringing up, guv'nor?

BLAKE: Foster. We shall want the seaplane for this trip.

TINKER: (*Astonished*) This trip? Why, where are we going?

BLAKE: To Saint Marguerite, of course, Tinker! To Saint Marguerite!

FADE IN of music.

FADE DOWN music.

FADE IN of a seaplane.

TINKER: What time is it, guv'nor?

BLAKE: It's about nine o'clock. We seem to be making pretty good time.

TINKER: I could do with a spot of grub, I know that much!

BLAKE: (*Amused*) I expect Tony will get you some breakfast when we … (*Suddenly excited*) Look!!! There we are, Tinker!

TINKER: (*After a tiny pause*) Phew! Is … Is that the castle?

BLAKE: That's the castle all right, Tinker.

TINKER: Blimey! I bet there isn't another place like this. Cor lumme, just look at those rocks!

BLAKE: (*Thoughtfully*) I'd better bring the plane down over the other side.

FADE IN the noise of the seaplane slightly louder as the machine turns.

TINKER: Does Tony Carradine live here all the time?

BLAKE: No. The place belongs to his uncle, Peter Marthioly. And from what I hear the old boy keeps a pretty tight hold on the family purse strings. Hold on, Tinker, we're going down now!

The engine slows down as the plane descends.

TINKER: There's a sort of jetty on the right … No, further over!

BLAKE: Don't worry … we'll make it!

The engine stops.

TINKER: (*Shouting*) I've got the rope …

BLAKE: (*Also shouting*) Pull, Tinker! Further over to the right! That's it! (*Rather breathless*) I should tie the rope pretty tight, Tinker.

TINKER: (*After a slight pause*) Funny nobody's come down to meet us. They must 'ave seen us land, don't you think so?

BLAKE: Perhaps.

TINKER: 'Tisn't exactly what you might call soothing around 'ere, is it? (*Shivering*) Proper gives you the creeps!

BLAKE: (*Laughing*) Come on, we'd better go up to the house.

TINKER: Yes … Yes. O.K.

FADE footsteps.

FADE IN the sound of TINKER hammering on the front door.

BLAKE: If you knock much louder, Tinker, you'll bring the castle down on top of us.

TINKER: Old Tony must be 'aving his beauty sleep!

5

BLAKE: (*Amused*) Yes.

TINKER: Crikey, if I had to stay long in this place it would … (*He hesitates*) What's up, guv'nor?

BLAKE: (*Seriously*) Listen!

TINKER: Someone coming?

BLAKE: Listen, Tinker!

As though drifting upon a gentle breeze, there is the far off music of pipes.

The music has an eerie, mournful cadence that somehow holds an oddly exotic quality.

TINKER: (*Astonished*) What is it …?

BLAKE: (*Thoughtfully*) I'm not sure, Tinker. I'm not sure …

TINKER: (*Suddenly*) There's someone coming!

The door opens.

ANGUS answers the door.

He is a very old man.

BLAKE: Good morning, my name …

ANGUS: Go away! Please go away! We don't want to see strangers today … This is a house of death … Go away! Please …

BLAKE: (*Quietly*) My name is Blake. Sexton Blake.

ANGUS: Sexton Blake! Sexton Blake, is it? Ye've come to a house of death, Mr Blake! (*Mumbling to himself*) Ye've come to a house of death! (*He continues to murmur to himself*)

BLAKE: (*Quietly*) Come along, Tinker, we'd better follow the old boy.

The door of the castle closes.

ANGUS: Wait here and I'll …

PETER MARTHIOLY arrives.

His voice is deep yet rather precise.

He is rather elderly.

PETER: What is it, Angus? You seem to be …
            (*Suddenly surprised at the sight of visitors*) Oh,
            er … good morning!

ANGUS: This is Mr Blake, sir.

PETER: Blake? Blake did you say?

BLAKE: Yes. Sexton Blake.

PETER: Sexton Blake! But what brings you here, sir?

BLAKE: I received a telegram from an acquaintance of
            mine asking me to come here. A rather urgent
            telegram.

PETER: An acquaintance, sir?

BLAKE: (*Softly*) Tony Carradine.

PETER: (*Astonished*) A telegram … from Tony?
            (*Suddenly*) Then I expect my nephew had a
            very good reason for inviting you here, Mr
            Blake.

They are crossing the hall towards the library.

PETER: Permit me to introduce myself. I am Tony's
            uncle, Peter Marthioly.

BLAKE: How do you do?

PETER: It's rather unfortunate that you should have
            picked this particular moment to pay us a visit,
            Mr Blake, you see my younger brother …
            Angelo … died last night. He fell from the
            window of his bedroom onto the rocks and …
            (*He falters, obviously distressed*)

BLAKE: (*After a tiny pause*) Was it … an accident?

PETER: (*Simply*) But of course. (*Aside*) Take Mr
            Blake's coat, Angus.

ANGUS: Yes, sir.

PETER: I need hardly tell you, of course, that this affair
            has given us all rather … we … well, to say the
            least, a nasty shock. Tony seems to have been
            completely knocked off his pedestal. He's got

some absurd story at the back of his mind about having seen the family ghost outside my brother's room.

BLAKE: You mean ... The Man in the Iron Mask?

PETER: Yes. Tony heard my brother scream apparently and immediately ... (*He hesitates*)

BLAKE: (*Quietly*) What is it?

PETER: I ... I thought I heard something ...

TINKER: Listen!

In the distant background the weird music is heard.
After a little while it fades.

PETER: (*Rather frightened*) Listen! (*Obviously terrified*) What is it ...? That music ... we heard it last night, and ...

BLAKE: You heard it ... last night?

PETER: Yes. Soon after dinner. We were all rather puzzled by it ... Tony seems to think that the music was over the other side of the lake. Sound travels rather ...

BLAKE: (*Quietly*) Had your brother always been here ... I mean at Saint Marguerite?

PETER: Why, no! He was abroad for ten years. Actually he only arrived home from North Borneo about a week ago. He was a government agent.

BLAKE: North Borneo? Not the Datu country, by any chance?

PETER: (*Surprised*) Why, yes! (*Puzzled*) How did you know?

There is a pause.

BLAKE: Mr Marthioly, what have you done about your brother?

PETER: I notified the local coroner. A doctor will be coming from Threwfell.

BLAKE: I see. And the police?

8

PETER:	(*Irritated*) The police? What right have the police to interfere? I tell you it was an accident! (*A slight pause*) I'm sorry, Mr Blake … forgive me, I … I shouldn't have lost my temper like that. As a matter of fact I do believe that Benito has sent for the police.
BLAKE:	Benito?
PETER:	My nephew. Angelo's son.
BLAKE:	Mr Marthioly … that music … the music we have just heard …
PETER:	(*Eagerly*) Yes …?
BLAKE:	When was the first time you heard it?
PETER:	Why, I told you … Last night … just after dinner … (*Alarmed*) Mr Blake, what is it? What is it?
BLAKE:	(*Quietly*) In the Datu country it is called The Song of Death …
PETER:	(*Softly*) The Song of Death …
BLAKE:	I should rather like to see your brother, if that is possible?
PETER:	Why, of course. I'll tell Angus to take you to his room. Perhaps you'll join me later in the library?
BLAKE:	Of course.
PETER:	(*Softly, bewildered*) The Song of Death …

FADE voices.

A pause.

A door opens.

PETER:	(*Slightly brighter*) You've been such a long time, Blake, I was beginning to wonder if … (*He hesitates*)
BLAKE:	(*Quietly*) Mr Marthioly, I'm afraid I've got some rather unpleasant news for you.

9

PETER: I … don't understand.

BLAKE: Your brother was … murdered.

PETER: Murdered! But … that's impossible!

BLAKE: I'm afraid there's no doubt about it, sir. The coroner will undoubtedly corroborate my statement. Your brother was strangled into unconsciousness long before he died.

PETER: Strangled! (*Softly, bewildered*) But … But this is dreadful … dreadful … You're quite sure that …

BLAKE: (*Softly*) Quite sure. And now, if you don't mind, I'd rather like to have a word with Tony Carradine.

PETER: Yes. Yes, I'll tell him … My word, it's a good job you're here, Mr Blake …

The library door closes.

TINKER: Crikey, he's got the wind up properly. Not that I blame him … I wonder what young Tony's got to say about all this!

BLAKE: We shall soon find out. Here he is, Tinker, unless I'm mistaken.

The door opens.

TONY CARRADINE arrives.

He is young and rather excitable.

TONY: Hello, Blake! Hello there, young Tinker!

BLAKE: Hello, Tony!

TONY: I've just seen my uncle. So Uncle Angelo <u>was</u> murdered, after all!

BLAKE: Yes. (*A pause*) Why did you send for me, Tony?

TONY: Blake … Someone had put the fear of death into my uncle. He was terrified out of his wits.

BLAKE: You mean, he was actually threatened?

10

TONY: Oh, no … not threatened. But … there was a ghost.

BLAKE: (*Pleasantly*) The Man in the Iron Mask?

TONY: It's no good smiling, Blake. I tell you I've seen him … Once when I sent you that telegram, and once … outside Uncle Angelo's room.

BLAKE: Last night?

TONY: Yes.

BLAKE: What happened?

TONY: I went to bed rather early. Pretty soon after dinner in fact. I'd been in bed about an hour or so when I heard a scream! My God, what a scream. For a second or two I was too damned scared to do anything, then I shot out of bed and into the corridor …

TINKER: Is that when you saw The Man in the Iron Mask?

TONY: Yes. He was coming out of Uncle Angelo's room. I could see him quite plainly, Blake.

BLAKE: Tony, why should anyone want to murder your uncle?

TONY: I don't know. (*Thoughtfully*) He was always so very kind.

BLAKE: Was he a wealthy man?

TONY: Not that I know of. Now if it had been Uncle Peter I could have …

The library door opens and BENITO enters.

He is rather an eccentric person and just at the moment extremely angry.

BLAKE: (*Sharply*) Who is this?

TONY: Benito, why … what's the matter?

BENITO: (*Extremely angry*) Where did you get this box?

TONY: (*Puzzled*) Benito … what on earth are you talking about?

11

BENITO:	You know perfectly well what I'm talking about! This box belonged to my father.
TONY:	(*Quietly*) I know that, Benito.
BENITO:	Then why should it be in your room?
TONY:	(*Puzzled*) In <u>my</u> room?
JOAN:	(*Rather breathless*) Let me explain, Tony …
TONY:	Why, hello Joan!
JOAN:	I found Benito in your room. He had this box in his hand and …
BENITO:	For God's sake stop beating about the bush!! I found this …
BLAKE:	(*Calmly*) An admirable suggestion.
BENITO:	Who … Who is this man?
TONY:	Oh … er … I'm sorry. My fiancée, Miss Dixon, and my cousin Benito Marthioly. Sexton Blake.
JOAN:	How do you do?
BENITO:	Sexton Blake! What are you doing here?
BLAKE:	Well, I'm not exactly here for the good of my health, Mr Marthioly, I can assure you. There seems to be a little excitement about the box you're holding.
BENITO:	(*Softly*) It belonged to my father. He kept some papers in it … important papers. He showed me the box the day he returned from Borneo and …
BLAKE:	Then you did not return from Borneo with your father?
BENITO:	No. I've lived here most of my life. (*Suddenly angry*) But all this is wasting time! I found this box in Tony's room and it's quite obvious what happened!
JOAN:	(*Softly*) What do you mean?
TONY:	(*Slowly*) What do you mean, Benito?

12

BENITO:	You murdered my father! You murdered him for … what was in this box!!!
TONY:	(*Furiously*) It's a lie! It's a damn lie!!!
JOAN:	Tony, please!
TINKER:	Take it easy, mate!
JOAN:	(*Softly*) You know perfectly well who murdered your father, Benito …
BENITO:	The Man in the Iron Mask? (*Scoffing*) A likely story, I must say!!!

The door opens.

TONY:	What is it, Angus?
ANGUS:	An Inspector MacTaggart has arrived, sir. I think he would rather like to have a word with Mr Blake.
BLAKE:	Yes, of course. Come along, Tinker.
ANGUS:	You'll find the Inspector in the Bay lounge, it's on the far side of the hall.
BLAKE:	Thank you. (*After a tiny pause*) We'll see you later, Tony.
TONY:	(*Obviously rather distressed*) Yes … Yes, all right.

The door closes.

A pause.

We hear the sound of footsteps on a parquet floor.

A pause.

TINKER:	I say, is this the way to the Bay lounge, guv'nor? It looks to me as if …
BLAKE:	Inspector MacTaggart can wait, Tinker. Just at the moment I'm rather anxious to have a look at the corridor upstairs …
TINKER:	You mean where Tony reckons he saw The Man in the Iron Mask?
BLAKE:	(*Quietly*) Yes.
TINKER:	O.K.

A pause.

BLAKE: There's certainly an atmosphere about this place … (*Suddenly*) Ah, here we are, Tinker!

TINKER: Is this the room? I thought it was the one at the end of the corridor?

BLAKE: No, this is it.

TINKER: What are you looking for, guv'nor?

BLAKE: (*Thoughtfully*) I'm looking for … some sort of … a panel, Tinker. I feel sure … there must … Hello, what's this?

TINKER: (*Amused*) It's only a crack in the woodwork. Doesn't go very deep.

BLAKE: M'm.

TINKER: These walls are pretty thick.

BLAKE: (*In the background*) I don't know whether they are or not …

TINKER: What do you think happened, guv'nor? Surely young Tony must 'ave been …

Suddenly part of the wall moves.

It is on a pivot and the movement is totally unexpected.

BLAKE: (*Suddenly*) Look out!

TINKER: (*Astonished*) Blimey, what's happened?

BLAKE: (*Amused*) Gosh! Look!

TINKER: (*Amazed*) Gosh! Look! A bit of the wall's moved!

BLAKE: (*Seriously*) Just as I expected.

TINKER: It's … It's an underground passage. Crikey, no wonder the ghost managed to disappear …

BLAKE: Come on, Tinker! Mind your head!

TINKER: 'Ave you got a match?

BLAKE: Wait until we get inside the … (*He is struggling through the opening*) Ah, that's better …

There is a slight pause.

14

Both TINKER and SEXTON BLAKE are now in the underground passage leading from the corridor.

TINKER: (*Excitedly*) Guv'nor! Guv'nor, where are you?

BLAKE strikes a match.

BLAKE: It's all right, Tinker – I'm here …

TINKER: (*Nervously*) Phew! Not exactly a blinkin' health resort, is it?

BLAKE: This corridor seems to be fairly long judging by … (*Suddenly*) What's that?

The wall slowly closes.

TINKER: (*Suddenly desperate*) Look, it's the wall … It's closing …

BLAKE: My God, we're trapped, Tinker!!!!

TINKER: (*Almost terrified*) Guv'nor, look!! Look!!!

BLAKE: What is it, Tinker?

TINKER: There's … There's someone at the end of the corridor …

BLAKE: At the end of … Yes! Yes … He's … He's coming towards us … Tinker … It's … It's the Man in the Iron Mask!!!!

TINKER: What … What's going to happen?

BLAKE: Don't move! As soon as he … (*He hesitates*)

TINKER: Guv'nor … What is it? (*Alarmed*) What is it?

BLAKE: Listen!

In the background can be heard the strange exotic music of the pipes.

TINKER: (*Terrified*) It's … that music!!!!

BLAKE: (*Softly*) The Song of Death.

The music can be heard, strange mournful music.

END OF EPISODE ONE

EPISODE TWO

SEXTON BLAKE
INVESTIGATES

OPEN TO:

ANNOUNCER: In Episode One of A Case For Sexton Blake, Blake and Tinker went to a lonely castle named Saint Marguerite in Northumberland, the home of the Marthioly family On arrival they found that Angelo, Peter Marthioly's younger brother, had been murdered and that The Man in the Iron Mask, the family ghost, had been seen during the night of the murder. While looking into the affair, Blake and Tinker are trapped in a secret passage.

FADE IN of music.

FADE DOWN music.

BLAKE: My God, we're trapped, Tinker!!!!

TINKER: (*Almost terrified*) Guv'nor, look!! Look!!!

BLAKE: What is it, Tinker?

TINKER: There's … There's someone at the end of the corridor …

BLAKE: At the end of … Yes! Yes … He's … He's coming towards us … Tinker … It's … It's the Man in the Iron Mask!!!!

TINKER: What … What's going to happen?

BLAKE: Don't move! As soon as he … (*He hesitates*)

TINKER: Guv'nor … What is it? (*Alarmed*) What is it?

BLAKE: Listen!

In the background can be heard the strange exotic music of the pipes.

TINKER: (*Terrified*) It's … that music!!!!

BLAKE: (*Softly*) The Song of Death.

The music can be heard, strange mournful music.

TINKER: (*Excitedly*) I say, guv'nor, look … he's hesitating.

BLAKE: He's heard the music, Tinker. (*Shouting*) Look out!

A shot is heard – it ricochets off the wall.

TINKER: (*Anxiously*) Are you all right?

BLAKE: Yes – keep down, Tinker.

A second shot is heard.

TINKER: Ghost or no ghost he's a pretty rotten shot!

BLAKE: Stay here … now don't move …

TINKER: (*Anxiously*) What are you going to do?

BLAKE: Don't move, Tinker!

TINKER: Don't get too near, guv'nor, or he'll …

Another shot is heard.

It strikes the wall near Tinker.

BLAKE: Our friend seems to be improving.

TINKER: (*Nervously*) Yes … I think perhaps you're right.

BLAKE: (*Suddenly*) I say, Tinker … look!

TINKER: Crikey, he's disappeared!

BLAKE: He can't have vanished into thin air … There must be some sort of an opening at the end of the passage. Come along, Tinker.

TINKER: Careful … it might be a trap!

BLAKE: Stand on the other side, just in case he fires again.

TINKER: No. You go over the other side, he's …

BLAKE: Do as I say, Tinker1

TINKER: O.K.!

A pause.

BLAKE: (*He hesitates*) M'm … he certainly seems to have disappeared.

TINKER: (*Nervously*) You … you don't think it was a ghost, do you, guv'nor?

BLAKE: Those bullets sounded pretty real to me, my boy, I don't know what you think! (*Intrigued by his surroundings*) I say, this passage is an amazing sort of place … it's obviously part of the catacombs …

TINKER: Yes, well we can't get out of here too soon for yours truly. Proper gives me the heeby-jeebys.

BLAKE: (*Thoughtfully*) I wonder what happened to our friend in the Iron Mask. He certainly made a very quick exit.

TINKER: That music seemed to do the trick. Got him properly rattled.

BLAKE: Yes. He was quite obviously puzzled by it.

BLAKE sounds slightly out of breath.

TINKER: What are you doing, guv'nor?

BLAKE: There's a rock over here. I was trying to force it. M'm. Not much hope I'm afraid.

TINKER: There must be quite a lot of ways in an' out of this place, if only….

BLAKE: Yes. But he seemed to be standing about here when … (*He hesitates*)

TINKER: What's up?

BLAKE: (*After a pause*) I thought I heard something … that's all.

A pause.

TINKER: Well, one thing we do know. Old Tony was telling us the truth all right when he said that he'd seen the Man in the Iron Mask.

BLAKE: M'm …

TINKER: (*Amused*) I say, MacTaggart must be getting a bit impatient. Don't forget we promised to join the old boy in the lounge.

21

BLAKE: I wonder what interesting theories
                Inspector MacTaggart has ... *(He
                hesitates – softly)* Listen, Tinker ... it's
                that music again.

The same strange rather eerie music can be heard.
It seems a very long distance away.

TINKER: Sounds to me as if it's coming from the
                end of the passage.

BLAKE: Yes. Yes, I think you're right.

A pause.

TINKER: What – what are we going to do?

BLAKE: Carry on. It's no good turning back
                because there may be someone in the
                corridor. In any case we might not be
                able to get the panel open.

TINKER: *(Apprehensively)* Yes, but ... where does
                this lead us to ...?

BLAKE: Well, by the sound of things it might
                lead us to the music ... and after that,
                Tinker, music hath charms. *(As an
                afterthought)* We hope ...

FADE IN of music.

Quick FADE DOWN of music.

MacTAGGART: *(Obviously very irritated)* It's extremely
                annoying ... it's extremely annoying to
                say the least! I particularly asked to see
                Mr Blake! I particularly ...

BENITO: It seems to me, my dear Inspector, that
                you're bothering your head far too much
                about Sexton Blake.

MacTAGGART: Is that so now?

BENITO:	This case is cut and dried. Tony murdered my father, and he murdered him for what was in this box!
MacTAGGART:	Ye seem to be forgetting that it was your cousin who sent for Sexton Blake.
BENITO:	I'm not forgetting anything! (*After a tiny pause*) It's quite obvious why Tony sent for Sexton Blake …

The door opens.

TONY:	(*Quietly*) I'm glad you think so, 'Nito.
BENITO:	(*Surprised*) Why … why, Tony! (*Suddenly*) You were listening! You were listening to every single word I …
TONY:	It was hardly necessary for me to listen, Benito. Your voice has quite a penetrating quality.
JOAN:	Don't argue with him, Tony … please! (*Suddenly, rather desperate*) Oh, 'Nito, can't you see that Tony had nothing to do with your father's death? Can't you see that the Man in the Iron …?
BENITO:	(*Scoffingly*) The Man in the Iron Mask! A likely story I must say!!!

The door opens rather suddenly.
It is obviously rather a surprise.

JOAN:	Angus! What … what is it?
BENITO:	(*Angry*) What is it …? What do you want?
ANGUS:	(*After a tiny pause*) I came to see the Inspector.
MacTAGGART:	Well?
ANGUS:	We don't seem to be able to find Sexton Blake, sir. Mr Marthioly is still searching.

MacTAGGART: Yes. Yes, all right, Thank you.

BENITO: (*Irritated*) All right, Angus ... you can go. (*Suddenly angry*) I said, you can go, Angus!

ANGUS: (*Slowly, almost ominously*) Have a care, Master Benito ... He who scoffs at the Man in the Iron Mask shall live to rue it!

BENITO: (*Furiously*) Get back to the kitchen, you insolent old fool!

ANGUS: (*Slowly*) Have a care, Master Benito. Angelo Marthioly died at the hands of the Man in the Iron Mask.

BENITO: (*Almost in a rage*) Get ... back ... to the kitchen!

There is a slight pause.

The door closes.

JOAN: (*Softly*) Benito ... you really should make some attempt to pull yourself together.

BENITO: (*Ignoring her*) Insolent old fool! If you want me, Inspector, I shall be in the library!

MacTAGGART: Very good, sir.

The door closes.

JOAN: I shouldn't attach too much importance to Benito, Inspector. The death of his father has naturally ... well ... unbalanced him a little.

MacTAGGART: Aye, well, that's one way of looking at it, Miss. (*Impatiently*) I wonder what the Dickens has happened to Sexton Blake?

JOAN: Well, he must be somewhere in the castle.

TONY:	Blake told us that he was coming straight here, Inspector, when he left the library.
MacTAGGART:	M'm …
JOAN:	I say, I … hope to goodness he's all right!
MacTAGGART:	Don't worry about Sexton Blake, miss. (*Chuckling*) He can take care of himself. (*A tiny pause*) Mr Carradine …
TONY:	Yes, Inspector?
MacTAGGART:	I should rather like to have a word with Angus. I was wondering …
TONY:	You'll find him in the servants' quarters. There's a door on the right of the staircase, you've probably seen it.
MacTAGGART:	Yes. I'll see ye both later.

TONY opens the door.

MacTAGGART:	Ah, thank ye, sir.

The door closes.

JOAN:	Tony …
TONY:	Yes, darling?
JOAN:	(*Hesitatingly*) Why does Benito hate you … so intensely?
TONY:	Probably because I used to get along so well with his father. We were very good friends, you know. Uncle Angelo and I …
JOAN:	Yes. Yes, I know.

There is a slight pause.

TONY:	Joan, you look worried. I do hope that this ghastly business hasn't … (*He hesitates*)

Somewhere, in the background of the room a noise is heard. It is SEXTON BLAKE and TINKER trying to find the hidden panel which serves as an entrance into the lounge.

JOAN: What … what is it?

TONY: (*Softly*) I don't know. It seems to me to be coming from behind the bookcase.

JOAN: But that's ridiculous, why …

TONY: (*An excited whisper*) Joan! Joan … look!

JOAN: What is it?

TONY: I saw the bookcase move …

JOAN: Don't be silly!

TONY: Honestly, darling, I'm … I'm not joking!

JOAN: Then there must be a sort of … secret passage. Perhaps that's how the Man in the Iron Mask manages to …

TONY: (*Excitedly*) It's moving, Joan! There's someone coming into the room!

The noise of the bookcase is heard.

JOAN: What are you going to do?

TONY: (*Excitedly*) Stand on one side, Joan!

JOAN: I'd better fetch the Inspector or …

TONY: No, no, it's all right. This chair ought to do the trick.

The bookcase is finally forced away from the wall.

TINKER: (*Surprised*) Well, blow me, guv'nor, if we …

The chair catches Tinker on the back of the head.

He falls forward.

JOAN utters a sudden scream.

TONY: (*Astonished*) It's – it's Tinker!

JOAN: (*Amazed*) And here's … Mr Blake!

BLAKE: (*Amused*) I told you to let me go first, Tinker.

TINKER: Phew! What … what hit me?

TONY: (*Embarrassed*) I'm … I'm awfully sorry, Tinker. Why, I never thought for one moment that it would …

TINKER: Oh, that's all right.

JOAN: (*Quietly*) Hadn't we better get the bookcase back into position again?

TONY: (*Away from 'mike'*) Blake, where does this lead to? What is it … a sort of underground passage?

BLAKE: Yes, it … (*Moving the bookcase*) We'll have to push harder, Tony.

The bookcase is now in position again.

BLAKE: Ah, that's done it. Yes, there's a passage, Tony … it runs right through the heart of the rock on which the castle is built. There must be literally dozens of them.

JOAN: But how did you find it?

BLAKE: (*With a smile*) Well, I had an idea that the ghost didn't exactly vanish into thin air, Miss Dixon.

TONY: (*Excitedly*) Blake, you – haven't <u>seen</u> the Man in the Iron Mask?

BLAKE: Yes. Yes, I've seen him. (*Suddenly*) Tony, would you mind telling Inspector MacTaggart that I'd like a word with him?

TONY: No, of course not. Come along, Joan.

The door opens and closes.

TINKER: (*Puzzled*) You know, guv'nor, the thing I can't understand about this business is the motive. Crikey, there must be a blinkin' motive. Angelo Marthioly wasn't bumped off just for the fun of the thing, now was he?

BLAKE: What about the contents of the deed box? According to our friend Benito there's the motive.

TINKER: Yes, but we've only his word for it. The deed box might always have been empty.

BLAKE: I don't think so, Tinker. You see, both
                Tony and Peter Marthioly agree with
                Benito on that point. There must have
                been something in the deed box to start
                with. Now if we can assume that … (*He
                hesitates*)

In the background there is the distant roll of thunder.

BLAKE: That sounds like thunder.

TINKER: Yes, I thought it looked stormy when …

The door is thrown open.

*In the background the sound of heavy knocking can be
heard.*

There is also a second roll of thunder.

PETER: (*Excitedly*) Mr Blake … would you mind
                coming into the hall, please?

BLAKE: No, of course not. What's happened?

PETER: We – we heard that music again … that
                strange, peculiar music. Then someone
                started banging on the door. I thought
                perhaps that, under the circumstances,
                both you and the Inspector would care to
                be present when …

BLAKE: (*Briskly*) Of course! Come along, Tinker!

FADE SCENE.

FADE IN various voices in the hall.
The knocking is now much louder.
Suddenly the voice of SIBOKU is heard.
He is demanding that the door is opened.
His voice is almost an hysterical wail.

JOAN: (*Alarmed*) Tony … what is it?

TONY: It's … it's all right, darling.

SEXTON BLAKE arrives with PETER MARTHIOLY.

28

MacTAGGART:	Hello, Blake … I've been looking all over the place for you!
PETER:	(*Shouting*) Open the door, Angus!

The heavy door is unbolted.
It gradually opens.
There is a third roll of thunder.
Then a sudden start of astonishment from JOAN.

JOAN:	It's … it's an Indian!
SIBOKU:	Where is my master? Where is Tuan Angelo?
BENITO:	(*Astonished*) Why – it's Siboku!
BLAKE:	You know this man?
BENITO:	But, of course … it's Siboku. My father's Datu servant.
TINKER:	Datu servant! Crikey, then that music we heard was …
BLAKE:	Quiet, Tinker … he'll hear you!
SIBOKU:	(*Quietly*) Siboku play Death Song … Siboku fear for Tuan Angelo …
BENITO:	Someone ought to tell the poor devil that …
BLAKE:	Yes. (*Softly*) Siboku … your master is dead.
SIBOKU:	Tuan Angelo … dead. Killed by Man in Iron Mask … killed by …
PETER:	(*Staggered*) Why … why, how did you know? (*Angry*) Speak up, you yellow devil, how did you know that …?
BLAKE:	(*Gently*) Mr Marthioly, please …
PETER:	I'm – I'm sorry.
BLAKE:	Yes, your master was killed by the Man in the Iron Mask, but tell me … how did you know this …?

SIBOKU:	Tuan Angelo fear Man in Iron Mask. He say that …
PETER:	But surely you don't believe this man – why, surely it's …
MacTAGGART:	I don't know. But if he is telling the truth it certainly opens up a lot o' new possibilities.
BLAKE:	(*Quietly*) Siboku … tell us what you know of the Iron Mask …
SIBOKU:	(*Alarmed*) Iron Mask … ayah Kipangu – Tig Ayah Kipangu!
MacTAGGART:	What's he saying, Blake?
BLAKE:	(*Slowly*) The Iron Mask is devil's magic … strong devil's magic …

There is a sudden crash of distant thunder …
SIBOKU utters a shriek.
He is alarmed by the storm.

PETER:	What's the matter with him?
BLAKE:	The poor devil's frightened. Come inside, Siboku. Take him across to the fire, Miss Dixon.
TINKER:	(*Excitedly*) Guv'nor …
BLAKE:	What is it, Tinker?
TINKER:	The storm's getting worse … we ought to do something about the plane. It's only moored with one rope and if the wind gets pretty bad then …
BLAKE:	Good lord! Yes! We can't afford to take any risk with that. MacTaggart, we'll join you later! Tinker and I must see if we can make the plane safe. It's on the lake.
MacTAGGART:	Right you are, Mr Blake.
TONY:	Can I give you a hand, Blake?

BLAKE: No, we'll manage all right. Come along, Tinker!

FADE SCENE.

FADE In of the storm.

The lake is obviously very rough and the seaplane is tossing about.

TINKER and SEXTON BLAKE are at work endeavouring to steady the plane.

BLAKE: (*Calling*) What's the rope like?

TINKER: (*In the background*) Pretty good … she should be all right if we can steady her.

BLAKE: I'll get some rocks. If we get her round towards the wind I can load the floats …

TINKER: Yes, O.K.

A pause.

TINKER and SEXTON BLAKE are now closer together.

We hear bumping sounds as BLAKE puts rocks on the floats.

BLAKE: I think that's all right. She seems pretty steady. Damn good job you remembered, Tinker. (*Casually*) Come along, we'd better get back.

TINKER: (*Softly*) Guv'nor … Look, he's …

BLAKE: Look out!!

A shot is heard.

The bullet whizzes past the seaplane and strikes a rock.

TINKER: It's the Man in the Iron Mask. Keep down, guv'nor.

BLAKE: We'll have to make a dash for it, Tinker. Quickly!

FADE UP of storm.

FADE IN of SEXTON BLAKE hammering on the heavy door.

BLAKE: Come on – open up.

The door opens.

BLAKE: Good! Are you all right, Tinker?

TINKER: (*Out of breath*) Yes … O.K. … guv'nor!

FADE the storm down as the door shuts.

JOAN: (*Excited*) Mr Blake … Siboku went wild … the storm frightened him … he ran away from us … the others are trying to find him.

BLAKE: Never mind Siboku, Miss Dixon! Which is the way to the roof?

JOAN: (*Surprised*) To the roof? Why, up the stairs near the library, but why on earth do …?

BLAKE: Come along, Tinker!

TINKER: Ready, guv'nor!

We hear hurrying steps.

FADE SCENE.

FADE IN TINKER and SEXTON BLAKE hurriedly climbing the staircase.

The sound of the storm draws nearer.

BLAKE: There's a door here, Tinker. Stand clear, I'm going to blow the lock.

Several revolver shots are heard.

BLAKE: Ah, that's done it!

The door is thrown open.

FADE IN of the storm.

TINKER: (*Excitedly*) There he is, guv'nor! There he is!

BLAKE: Stand back!

There is a sudden shot and the unexpected smashing of glass.

BLAKE: He's hit the fanlight. Now keep down, Tinker, for heaven's sake!

TINKER: (*Softly*) He's over on the other side near the chimney. Look out!!!

There is a second shot which once again strikes the door.

BLAKE: We'd better split up. I'll join you on the far side of the chimney.

TINKER: Yes … yes, all right. And watch your napper, guv'nor!

BLAKE: You watch yourself, young Tinker!

There is a pause.

The storm is heard.

The rain and thunder growing steadily worse.

Someone gives a soft whistle.

TINKER: (*Quietly*) Is … that you, guv'nor?

BLAKE: Yes. What's happened?

TINKER: I don't know. He seems to have done a bunk all right. Blimey, this bloke seems to do the Indian rope trick an' the disappearing act all in one. (*Suddenly*) I say … what about the chimney? You don't think that …

BLAKE: The chimney? It's one of those medieval affairs by the looks of things. Wait a minute, Tinker, I've got a torch somewhere if only … Oh, here we are! (*A tiny pause*) By jingo, Tinker … you're right. This is the way he's gone all right. Look!

TINKER: Crikey!

BLAKE: You can see where his feet have scraped away the soot.

TINKER: He's certainly got a nerve!

BLAKE: I don't know, those rungs look pretty safe. Stand on one side, Tinker!

TINKER: Crikey, you're not … (*Suddenly*) 'Ere, steady on … I'm going first.

BLAKE: No. Follow me … and don't take your weight off one rung until you've actually got another under your foot.

33

We hear scrambling sounds.

BLAKE: Careful!

Both SEXTON BLAKE and TINKER are entering the chimney.

When they speak their voices have a strange hollow sound.

TINKER: Steady on …

BLAKE: I'm all right. (*He is calling back*) The chimney curves to the left, Tinker … watch it!

TINKER: O.K.

BLAKE: (*After a pause*) It's pretty dark down here … I'm going to strike a match.

TINKER: What about the torch?

BLAKE: Too bright … (*He strikes a match*)

A pause.

TINKER: (*Calling*) Can you see anything?

BLAKE: Yes … the chimney branches into two parts. It's wider just here, that's how …

TINKER: (*Calling*) Did you hear that, guv'nor?

From above, and dominating even the muffled roar of the storm, comes the sudden crash of falling masonry.

There is a gigantic explosion.

BLAKE: (*Desperately*) Look out! Look out, Tinker!

TINKER: (*Bewildered*) What is it? What's happened?

There is another tremendous explosion which literally shakes the castle.

BLAKE: My God! We've walked into a trap, Tinker. He's dynamiting the chimney!

There is a third explosion almost as BLAKE finishes speaking.

BLAKE: Hold on, Tinker! Hold on!

Another explosion shatters almost the entrance to the chimney.

The noise of the falling masonry is deafening.

BLAKE: Hold on, Tinker! Hold on!

From somewhere below them a grim determined chuckle is heard.
It is the Man in the Iron Mask.
FADE IN of closing music.

END OF EPISODE TWO

EPISODE THREE

MENACE
AT THE MILL

OPEN TO:

ANNOUNCER: Sexton Blake and Tinker have been investigating the strange case of the murder of Angelo Marthioly, Peter Marthioly's younger brother, and Blake has come to the conclusion that The Man in the Iron Mask, the family ghost, conceals the identity of the murderer. At the end of the last episode, Blake and Tinker had been close on the heels of the mysterious figure and had pursued him down one of the castle of Saint Marguerite's ancient chimneys. When half way down a tremendous explosion occurred and Blake realised that the Man in the Iron Mask was dynamiting the chimney above them.

FADE IN of music.

FADE DOWN of music.
FADE IN an explosion and the noise of falling masonry.

BLAKE: (*Calling*) Hold on! Hold on, Tinker!

There is a second explosion.
This is followed by the noise of falling masonry.

TINKER: Look out, guv'nor!!

BLAKE: (*Shouting*) Drop, Tinker … drop, it's our only chance.

TINKER: O.K., guv'nor!!

Another explosion is heard.
FADE SCENE.

FADE IN the music of The Song of Death.
FADE music.

A door opens and closes.

JOAN: (*Obviously worried*) Oh, Inspector … I'm so glad you've come … where is everybody?

MacTAGGART: Looking for that confounded Indian, I expect. You look a bit done in, miss. If I were you, I should take things easy.

JOAN: I do wish Tony would …

The door opens.

JOAN: Tony! Are … are you all right?

TONY: Of course I'm all right, darling! Look here, you'd better have a spot of brandy or something!

MacTAGGART: Blake's a devil of a time messing about with that plane of his! I should have thought …

JOAN: Oh, but Mr Blake isn't outside, Inspector!

MacTAGGART: (*Surprised*) He isn't?

JOAN: No. Both Mr Blake and Tinker came back to the castle shortly after Siboku disappeared. They both seemed rather excited.

MacTAGGART: But – but where are they?

JOAN: Well, Mr Blake wanted to know how to reach the roof so I …

MacTAGGART: The roof!! The roof … did ye say?

TONY: (*Excited*) Look here, Inspector, they must have seen something happening up there while they were outside.

MacTAGGART: Yes. Come along, Mr Carradine, we …

The INSPECTOR is interrupted by the second explosion of the previous scene.

It is in the background.

TONY: My God, what's that?

MacTAGGART: It sounded to me as if the chimney was …

There is the third explosion and the distant noise of falling masonry.

JOAN: (*Alarmed*) Tony … Look! The fireplace, Tony … look!!

Parts of the falling masonry drop into the fireplace.

MacTAGGART: Great Scot, there's someone coming down it by the look of … It's Mr Marthioly!

TONY: (*Astonished*) Uncle Peter!!

PETER: (*Desperately*) Stand away! For God's sake stand …

There is a tremendous thud as SEXTON BLAKE and TINKER fall into the room.

MacTAGGART: Mr … Blake!!

A second later and yet another lot of dislodged masonry falls.

BLAKE: Get away from the fireplace, Tinker!

A slight pause.

TINKER: Phew! Are … are you o.k., guv'nor?

BLAKE: Yes … Mr Marthioly looks pretty bad … I should sit down, sir, if …

MacTAGGART: (*Suddenly exasperated*) Would some-body mind telling me, please, what the hell has been happening around here?

BLAKE: May we have your story first, Mr Marthioly?

TONY: You look tired, uncle, perhaps …

PETER: No. No, I'm all right, Tony. (*A tiny pause*) Well, I was searching the upper floors for Siboku when the idea occurred to me that he might possibly be on the

41

	roof. When I reached the roof, however, the first thing I saw was … The Man in the Iron Mask …
TONY:	(*Staggered*) The Man in the Iron Mask?
PETER:	Yes. I owe you an apology, Tony. I'm afraid that like Benito I was rather sceptical.
BLAKE:	Please go on, Mr Marthioly …
PETER:	Well, apart from the iron mask he was dressed in a long black cloak and was, in fact, exactly as Tony described him. He was standing on the far side of the roof near the chimney, and rather cautiously I made my way across the roof towards him. Suddenly, without the slightest warning, he disappeared. I stood still for a second or two … rather bewildered. The next thing I remember was being hit on the back of the head.
MacTAGGART:	And you didn't really see who it was that attacked you?
PETER:	No, I'm afraid not. And when I came round I was feeling too damn bad to worry about it. Besides, it was dark and I couldn't for the life of me think where I was, or what I was doing.
TONY:	Then what happened?
PETER:	I heard a voice. It was Mr Blake's, I believe. He said something about the chimney curving over to the left … then a match was struck … I could see the flame about twenty or thirty feet above me … and I knew then what had happened. That devil had obviously

	heaved me over the side of the chimney. I could see by the light of the match that I was on some sort of a ledge. It had been used by the old sweeps, I should imagine, as a sort of foothold. And I must have fallen on to it. I was just on the verge of shouting to Mr Blake when … when the explosion occurred.
BLAKE:	(*Quietly*) And what happened then?
PETER:	Well, I heard you shouting to Tinker, and for some reason or other that gave me more confidence. When the next explosion occurred I made a jump for it …
MacTAGGART:	Well, ye've certainly had a close shave!
PETER:	Well, I can tell you one thing, Inspector, I sincerely hope …

The door opens.

JOAN:	(*Softly*) Benito …
BENITO:	Why! What's – what's been happening?
TONY:	Perhaps you'll be interested to know that … Uncle Peter has been attacked …
BENITO:	Attacked …?
TONY:	Yes.
BENITO:	But … but by who …?
TONY:	By … The Man in the Iron Mask.
BENITO:	(*Alarmed*) No! No, I don't believe it! I don't believe it!!
PETER:	(*Quietly*) It's true, Benito.

There is a slight pause.

BENITO:	What – what are you all looking at me like that for …?
BLAKE:	Where have you been during the past twenty minutes?

BENITO:	You know perfectly well where I've been … looking for Siboku.
BLAKE:	Alone?
BENITO:	Why, yes of course I was … (*He stops*) Why do you ask? Why do you ask?
BLAKE:	I've rather got into the habit of asking questions, Mr Benito. You must forgive me if I sound a little inquisitive. Ah, here's Angus.
ANGUS:	(*Slowly*) You want me, Mr Blake?
BLAKE:	Yes, I wanted …
ANGUS:	If it's an alibi you're wanting, Mr Detective, then I'll be disappointing ye. I was looking for that yellow skinned devil Siboku … and I was alone … quite alone. (*He commences to chuckle*)
PETER:	(*Angry*) That will do, Angus!

ANGUS stops chuckling.
He is staring at PETER.

ANGUS:	What's the matter with you? Why are you covered in that awful …?
PETER:	I've been attacked … attacked by The Man in the Iron Mask.
ANGUS:	(*Staggered*) You!! You, master? (*Softly*) Then the curse falls upon the head of the house!
MacTAGGART:	(*Amazed*) Here, just a minute, my man! If you don't mind I'd …
ANGUS:	(*Ignoring him*) To look upon the mask of death … certain death.
PETER:	(*Annoyed*) Stop that stupid talk, Angus … and get my bath ready … I'm absolutely filthy. Oh, and I'm sure that

44

	Mr Blake and his assistant would … (*He stops*)

There is a knock on the door.

TONY:	What's that …?
JOAN:	There's someone at the door …
BLAKE:	Open it!

The door opens.

JOAN:	(*Surprised*) Siboku!
SIBOKU:	(*Hesitatingly*) Siboku … get lost … Siboku frightened … thunder devils … bad magic …
BENITO:	But where have you been? We've been looking all over the place for you …
SIBOKU:	(*Weakly*) Siboku … frightened … he get lost …
TONY:	(*Alarmed*) Look out! The poor devil's going to faint!!
BENITO:	I've got him!
PETER:	Get some brandy, Angus!
BLAKE:	(*Quietly*) No … no, he'll be all right. Let him rest on the sofa for a little while.
JOAN:	I'll get a rug for the poor man. I shouldn't be surprised if he doesn't have a nervous breakdown, what with one thing and another.
MacTAGGART:	(*Exasperated*) A nervous breakdown did ye say, miss? I shall be having a fit of hysterics unless somebody turns up with an alibi. Don't you realise that there isn't a single one of ye that can prove where ye were and what you were doing when Mr Peter was attacked?
PETER:	I say, look here, Inspector! You can't go about accusing …

45

BLAKE:	(*Suddenly*) Mr Marthioly, I think you said something about a bath?
PETER:	Er – oh yes, of course. Angus, show Mr Blake and his assistant to the north bedroom. The bathroom is next door.
BLAKE:	Thank you. See you later, Inspector. (*START FADE*) Come along, Tinker! Let's try and get rid of some of this soot!

FADE SCENE.

FADE IN of INSPECTOR MacTAGGART's voice.

MacTAGGART:	(*FADING IN*) Well, now, Mr Blake, I've been spending the last ten minutes or so going over in me mind the various suspects.
BLAKE:	(*Pleasantly*) Have you, Inspector? Pass me that brush, Tinker! Thanks. And what conclusion have you come to?
MacTAGGART:	Well now, it seems to me that the person who attacked Mr Marthioly must be one of three people. Either Benito … the old man Angus, or that Indian devil Siboku.
BLAKE:	M'm …
TINKER:	Yes, but look here, Inspector, we saw all those people after the attack and none of them were smothered in soot like the guv'nor and me. Now how the Dickens can you …
BLAKE:	Don't forget the cloak, Tinker, and the iron mask, too. That would keep the wearer fairly clean.
TINKER:	(*Thoughtfully*) Yes. Yes, I suppose it would. I never thought of that …

BLAKE:	You know, Inspector … the clothes brush, please, Tinker. Thanks … I can't quite see why you omit Peter Marthioly from your list of – er – possible suspects?
MacTAGGART:	Mr Marthioly? Why dammit, man, he's just been attacked by The Man in the Iron Mask. (*Suspiciously*) Look here, Blake, what are you getting at?
BLAKE:	I'm simply getting at the fact that in a case like this I don't think anyone should be ruled out as a possible suspect. After all, MacTaggart, we didn't actually see Peter Marthioly being attacked, now did we?
MacTAGGART:	No. No, I suppose not.
TINKER:	(*Excitedly*) Crikey, then you really think Peter Marthioly might …
BLAKE:	Might be the Man in the Iron Mask? Yes … just as it might be Benito … or Angus … or, of course, Siboku.
MacTAGGART:	M'm …
BLAKE:	It seems to me, Inspector, that we should concentrate more upon the motives for the crime, rather than the identity of the murderer. Why was Angelo Marthioly murdered? When we know the answer to that question, we shall know which of our four suspects is The Man in the Iron Mask.
MacTAGGART:	Aye, maybe you're right.
BLAKE:	Personally, I feel that if we could find the missing contents of the document

box, then the motive for the murder would be pretty obvious.

MacTAGGART: M'm. (*Suddenly*) Tinker said something about a hidden passage a little while ago. I was wondering if ...

BLAKE: Oh, yes. It starts from the corridor near Angelo's bedroom. After you've gone about thirty yards there's a fork ... we've only had a chance of investigating one side of it, so I think it might be quite a good idea if we gave the other the 'once over' ... What do you say, Inspector?

MacTAGGART: By all means ... by all means, Mr Blake!

BLAKE: Don't forget the torch, Tinker.

TINKER: O.K. ... guv'nor.

FADE SCENE.

FADE IN of the wall moving.

It stops.

BLAKE: There we are, Inspector. After you ...

MacTAGGART: (*Staggered*) Good lord ... how on earth did ye discover this ...?

BLAKE: (*Laughing*) Mind your head, Tinker ...

They enter the concealed passage.

MacTAGGART: (*Nervously*) Is – is this where ye both ... er ... saw The Man in the Iron Mask?

BLAKE: It is, Inspector ...

MacTAGGART: M'm ... er ... m'm ...

TINKER: What are you looking for, guv'nor?

BLAKE: I'm just looking ... for ... ah, here we are!

The wall closes.

MacTAGGART: (*Alarmed*) Look!! The wall ... it's closing! My God, Blake, we're ...

BLAKE:	(*Amused*) It's all right, there's nothing to get worried about. You see this slab? Well, as soon as you put any weight on it, it closes the entrance.
TINKER:	Then … that's what happened before?
BLAKE:	Yes … I'm afraid so, Tinker …
MacTAGGART:	I – er – suppose we can – er – get out of here all right, Blake?
BLAKE:	(*Amused*) I think so, Inspector. Ready …?
MacTAGGART:	Yes.
BLAKE:	I'll go first. Tinker … you follow the Inspector …
TINKER:	Righto.

There is a long pause.

We hear footsteps.

MacTAGGART:	(*Obviously rather nervous*) This isn't – er – exactly my cup of tea, I'm afraid.

There is another pause.

We hear more footsteps.

TINKER:	(*Excitedly*) 'Ere we are! This is where we turned off last time. We went round to the left.
BLAKE:	Yes. There's a panel on the left … it leads into the library … Steady, Tinker!
TINKER:	Crikey, this is on a bit of a slope.
BLAKE:	All right, MacTaggart?
MacTAGGART:	Yes … I'm all right.

There is a further pause.

And more footsteps are heard.

BLAKE:	There's some steps here! Flash the torch!

They are descending the steps.

TINKER:	O.K.?
MacTAGGART:	Bit slippy, aren't they?

BLAKE:	M'm – we must be well below the lake by now.
MacTAGGART:	Shall we – er – carry on?
BLAKE:	Oh yes, we want to find out where this leads to.
MacTAGGART:	I should think it's the half-way house to Hades by the look o' things.

TINKER laughs.
FADE slightly.

FADE UP of footsteps.

BLAKE:	Tired, Inspector?
MacTAGGART:	(*Rather breathless*) Yes … I feel a bit done in, you know.
TINKER:	It was funny how we started to climb uphill again. I wonder where the devil we are.
BLAKE:	I've got a feeling we're right over on the other side of the lake.
MacTAGGART:	The other side? You mean near Cawtry's Mill? I suppose that's possible …
TINKER:	(*Quietly*) I say, guv'nor …
BLAKE:	What is it, Tinker?
TINKER:	There looks to me to be a sort of trap door just above our heads. No, over here!
MacTAGGART:	Yes … the youngster's right, Blake!
BLAKE:	See if you can move it, Tinker. I'll give you a hand.
TINKER:	O.K.!

A slight pause.

MacTAGGART:	(*Excitedly*) He's moving it all right …
TINKER:	(*Straining on BLAKE's shoulders*) I shan't be … long if once …

Suddenly the trap door falls open.

TINKER:	That's done it …
BLAKE:	Carry on, Tinker. You go first.

BLAKE and MacTAGGART follow TINKER through the trap door.

MacTAGGART:	Phew, bit of a tight squeeze … Where the devil are we …?
BLAKE:	I don't know. Let's have …
MacTAGGART:	(*Suddenly*) Well, bless my soul!!!!
BLAKE:	What is it?
MacTAGGART:	Why – why look where we are! We're in Cawtry's Mill.
BLAKE:	Are you sure?
MacTAGGART:	Good heaven's yes! I've played around this place many a time when I was a youngster.
TINKER:	(*In the background*) He's right, guv'nor. Look … you can see the Castle from here …
MacTAGGART:	This is obviously the lower part of the windmill. I should imagine that …
BLAKE:	(*Softly*) A tunnel from the Castle to Cawtry's Mill. That's interesting, to say the least.
TINKER:	(*Excited*) There's a ladder over here, guv'nor! We can get to the top if we want to.
BLAKE:	Come along, Inspector, we might as well have a look around.
MacTAGGART:	Well, I'm not exactly intrigued at the thought of climbing to the top of a windmill, Blake.
BLAKE:	You'll be all right.

FADE SCENE slightly.

We hear climbing sounds.
FADE IN.

TINKER: Give us your hand, Inspector. That's
                   done it!

MacTAGGART: (*Breathless*) This – this … is …the loft,
                   isn't it?

BLAKE: Yes.

TINKER: Hello. What's the matter, guv'nor?

BLAKE: I was just looking at this straw.
                   Someone's been sleeping here, and quite
                   recently, too, I should imagine.

MacTAGGART: Yes.

BLAKE: (*Removing some of the straw*) Hello,
                   what's this? (*Suddenly amused*) Oh! Oh!

TINKER: What is it?

MacTAGGART: Looks like a club of some sort.

BLAKE: No. No, they're pipes. Datu pipes.

TINKER: Crikey, then Siboku must 'ave been here,
                   guv'nor.

BLAKE: Looks very much like it, Tinker.

MacTAGGART: (*Bewildered*) Ye mean to say you can get
                   music out of that thing?

BLAKE: Well, Siboku certainly does. So I don't
                   see why we shouldn't.

BLAKE commences to play the pipes.
It is the music of the Datu country.

TINKER: (*Excitedly*) That's it! That's it, guv'nor!

The music continues.
Suddenly it is interrupted by the crashing of the ladder.

MacTAGGART: (*Alarmed*) What's that?

TINKER: It's the ladder … look!!!

BLAKE: Yes. Yes, it's fallen.

MacTAGGART: Strewth, now we're in a pretty kettle of
                   fish an' no mistake.

Suddenly, from the background, comes the insane laughter of The Man in the Iron Mask.

MacTAGGART: My God, Blake … listen!

TINKER: (*Suddenly*) Guv'nor, we're trapped. He's set the mill on fire.

BLAKE: Yes! Yes, Tinker's right … Look down there, MacTaggart!

FADE IN of the crackle of fire devouring the lower part of the mill.

MacTAGGART: (*Almost desperate*) We've got to think fast this time, Blake. An' no mistake. My God, look at those flames … just look!!

FADE IN louder the noises of the fire.

VOICE: (*Booming from the background*) D'you hear me, Blake? This is The Man in the Iron Mask …

BLAKE: (*Suddenly angry*) I hear you, my friend! And I'll get you for this! Get you if it takes twenty years!

THE MAN IN THE IRON MASK laughs.

VOICE: Think fast, Sexton Blake! Think fast!

FADE DOWN the laughter.

FADE IN of the fire, and it is now spreading very quickly.

TINKER: (*Desperately*) What are we going to do, guv'nor? What are we going to do!!!?

FADE IN of closing music.

END OF EPISODE THREE

EPISODE FOUR

THE MAN
IN THE IRON MASK

OPEN TO:

ANNOUNCER: At the end of episode three, Blake, Tinker and MacTaggart were trapped in the blazing windmill, which has been set on fire by the Man in the Iron Mask. Listen now to what follows!

FADE IN of music.

FADE DOWN of music.
FADE IN of the crackle of fire devouring the lower part of the mill.

MacTAGGART: (*Almost desperate*) We've got to think fast this time, Blake. An' no mistake. My God, look at those flames … just look!!

FADE IN louder the noises of the fire.

VOICE: (*Booming from the background*) D'you hear me, Blake? This is The Man in the Iron Mask …

BLAKE: (*Suddenly angry*) I hear you, my friend! And I'll get you for this! Get you if it takes twenty years!

THE MAN IN THE IRON MASK laughs.

VOICE: Think fast, Sexton Blake! Think fast!

FADE DOWN the laughter.

FADE IN of the fire, and it is now spreading very quickly.

TINKER: (*Desperately*) What are we going to do, guv'nor? What are we going to do!!!?

BLAKE: Well, the first thing we are going to do is to let a bit of decent air into this place. Break those windows.

There is a sudden smashing of glass.

BLAKE: Ah, that's better!

MacTAGGART: I don't like the look o' this, Blake … an' that's putting it mildly, to be sure …

TINKER: If only there were sails on this blinkin' mill we might be able to do something.

BLAKE: (*Rather perturbed*) We've got to move fast, Tinker …

BLAKE is struggling with the thatching on the roof.

MacTAGGART: (*Coughing*) This … this damned fire is spreading.

BLAKE: Give me a hand with this … this … (*He continues to struggle*)

MacTAGGART: What the devil are ye … (*Still coughing*) … are ye doing?

BLAKE: I'm trying to make an opening in the roof … if we can once get on to the roof there may be a chance …

TINKER: 'Ere let me do that, guv'nor.

BLAKE: I'll hoist you up, Tinker! Perhaps if you …

MacTAGGART: Get on my shoulders … Come on, for gawd's sake jump to it!

There is a sudden crash as part of the downstairs gives way.

MacTAGGART: Did ye hear that? The lower floor's falling in. Come on, Tinker …

TINKER: (*Coughing rather badly*) It's … it's the smoke … I can't see very well, an' …

BLAKE: I've made a hole. Hoist him up, MacTaggart!!

MacTAGGART: Come on, lad!

TINKER: (*Coughing*) O … K …

BLAKE: Scramble through on to the roof if you can, Tinker!

TINKER: Yes … all … all right, guv'nor!

TINKER pulls the thatching away from the roof.

BLAKE: That's better! Good boy, Tinker …
                through you go!!

The thatching gives way and TINKER scrambles on to the roof.

A slight pause.

BLAKE: All right, Tinker?

TINKER: (*Excitedly*) Guv'nor, there's a bit of a
                pond over on the other side of the mill.
                One of us might be able to make a dive
                for it!

BLAKE: Stay where you are, Tinker. Come on,
                MacTaggart … up you get!

MacTAGGART: (*Exhausted*) I'll – I'll never be able to get
                up there, Blake, it's far better that you –

BLAKE: Come on, MacTaggart … none of that
                nonsense …

MacTAGGART: (*Breathing heavily*) You go first an' then
                perhaps …

His words are cut short by the sudden collapse of the downstairs structure.

BLAKE: That's the lower floor gone completely.
                Come on, MacTaggart, do as I say or by
                golly … Give him a hand, Tinker! That's
                better.

The INSPECTOR is struggling through the opening on to the roof.

TINKER: Are you all right?

MacTAGGART: Yes … yes, I'm all right. Phew, thank
                goodness for a breath of fresh air!

TINKER: Come on, guv'nor! Steady on the left,
                it's not too … that's better.

BLAKE is now on the roof.

BLAKE: Feel better, Inspector?

MacTAGGART:	Yes … Sorry I was such a nuisance, Blake.
BLAKE:	Oh, that's all right. Where's the pond you … (*A tiny pause*) Is … is that what you mean?
TINKER:	Yes. (*Excitedly*) It's all right, guv'nor, I could make it easy enough. Why, with a bit o' luck …
MacTAGGART:	Good God, man, we couldn't dive into that damn thing. We're about fifty feet up here and yon's nothing better than a puddle.
TINKER:	It's a chance anyway, an' that's more than we've got stuck up here. Another ten minutes an' the blinkin' mill will be burnt to a cinder!
BLAKE:	He's right, Inspector …
MacTAGGART:	But what about climbing down?
BLAKE:	No … we wouldn't have a dog's chance … not with a fire like this …
MacTAGGART:	But – but what if there's only a couple o' feet of mud in that pond an' nothing else? Why, God bless my soul, the first man to dive would …
BLAKE:	We've got to take that risk, MacTaggart. Hold my jacket, Tinker …
TINKER:	Look here, guv'nor, I spotted this blinkin' pond first, it's only right …
BLAKE:	I'll give you a shout if everything's all right …
MacTAGGART:	(*Anxiously*) For God's sake watch yourself, Blake …
BLAKE:	Don't worry, I'll be all right. Well … here goes!

There is a slight pause, then SEXTON BLAKE dives – a pause.

He hits the water with a resounding thud.

A pause.

The water ripples as BLAKE emerges.

BLAKE:	(*Shouting*) All right, you two … take it easy … There's about six feet of water and … (*Laughing*) tons of mud!!
TINKER:	Shall I go next, sir?
MacTAGGART:	(*Nervously*) Aye …
TINKER:	Can you dive, Inspector?
MacTAGGART:	Can I … (*Suddenly*) Well, it's a fine time o' day to start putting doubts into me head. Jump to it, laddie!
TINKER:	All right … here's my jacket … throw them all down before you jump for it.
MacTAGGART:	Aye … all right … only let's get this over with …
TINKER:	Well … Bob's your uncle!

TINKER dives.

A pause.

He hits the pond and a little while later joins SEXTON BLAKE.

BLAKE:	Good boy! How's MacTaggart … is he nervous?
TINKER:	Yes. I think he is a bit.
BLAKE:	He's throwing the coats down.
TINKER:	It's all right. I've got them!

TINKER catches the jackets.

A slight pause.

BLAKE:	MacTaggart seems to be hesitating.
TINKER:	(*Suddenly*) Here he comes!! Blimey, a bit flat, isn't it?

The INSPECTOR strikes the pond with a resounding thud.

BLAKE:	(*Laughing*) O.K. … Inspector …?
MacTAGGART:	(*Breathless*) I will be when I can get the confounded mud out of my … eyes … Ah well, I'm not sorry that's over!

At this moment the mid-structure of the mill, eaten away by the flames, collapses.

TINKER:	Crikey! Look at the mill!
MacTAGGART:	That's certainly a narrow squeak. We shouldn't have stood much chance if we'd still been up on the top!
BLAKE:	(*Quietly*) No, we shouldn't … I'm inclined to agree with you, Inspector. Incidentally, it doesn't look as if we shall be able to get back through the tunnel … not from this side of the mill.
MacTAGGART:	Aye …
TINKER:	I wonder what's been happening at the Castle?
MacTAGGART:	Well, nothin' out of the ordinary I hope. I left Benito, Angus, Siboku and Mr Peter Marthioly in separate rooms. So if …
BLAKE:	(*Interested*) M'm … anyone in charge?
MacTAGGART:	Yes. Holly. Sergeant Holly. I don't know whether you remember him or not, sir?
BLAKE:	Yes, I think so, Inspector. (*Thoughtfully*) How long has he been down here?
MacTAGGART:	He came down with me. He's a good man … Holly. Wee bit impatient at times, perhaps.
BLAKE:	Did you give him any instructions before we left?
MacTAGGART:	Yes, I told him to visit each room at regular intervals so that if anyone did

	leave them … (*Suddenly*) I say, it's just dawned on me. If one of the four suspects <u>is</u> … the Man in the Iron Mask … Holly must have had a pretty rough trip.
TINKER:	He'd certainly be in for it if that mad devil got his hands on him!
BLAKE:	Yes, I'm afraid so. Of course, now that we've discovered that the tunnel leads to Cawtry's Mill, we must bear in mind the fact that practically anyone could enter the Castle.
MacTAGGART:	Well, that's a cheery thought!
BLAKE:	On the other hand no one would enter the Castle without a reason, and certainly no one would murder Angelo Marthioly without a motive.
MacTAGGART:	But what <u>was</u> the motive?
BLAKE:	That's what we've got to find out, Inspector. (*Suddenly*) Yes, and the quicker we get back to the Castle, the better I shall like it. I've got a nasty sort of feeling about Saint Marguerite.
TINKER:	Yes, but how are we going to get back, guv'nor? It's half a mile at least to the headland, and we certainly shan't be able to get a boat from anywhere else.
BLAKE:	Well, in that case we'll have to swim across the lake. With a bit of luck we ought to do it in ten minutes.
MacTAGGART:	Not me! My swimming days are over, Blake. In any case I always needed a pretty extravagant start to finish a length!

BLAKE: (*Amused*) All right, MacTaggart, we'll see you
            later. Ready, Tinker?

TINKER: Yes, I'm ready, guv'nor. Hope you enjoy the
            walk, Inspector.

*There is a splash when SEXTON BLAKE and then TINKER
enter the lake.*
FADE SCENE.

TONY: I'm sorry to put you to all this trouble, darling.

JOAN: Don't be silly, Tony, it's no trouble. Although I
            certainly envy the servants being away from
            this terrible place.

TONY: Here's the coffee, dear. I should put the
            sandwiches on the tray.

JOAN: Yes. (*After a tiny pause*) Tony … do you think
            Sexton Blake and Tinker will find anything, I
            mean …

TONY: I don't know, darling, I'm sure. But if I were
            you I should just try and forget things for a
            little while.

JOAN: I keep telling myself that this Man in the Iron
            Mask is some outsider … some crazy killer that
            has found his way into the Castle. And yet … I
            know that isn't true. I know that it must be
            either Uncle Peter … Benito … Angus … or
            Siboku … or …

TONY: Darling, do try and take things easy. Whoever
            the Man in the Iron Mask is nothing can happen
            at the moment, so …

JOAN: (*Suddenly*) Why do you say that?

TONY: Well, Joan, everybody in the house except you
            and I are in separate rooms. And besides,
            Sergeant Holly has got instructions to look in
            on each of them at regular intervals. Now

surely the guilty person wouldn't be so stupid as to throw suspicion on to himself by leaving his room … not at a time like this.

JOAN: No, I suppose not.

TONY: Come along, dear, or the poor old sergeant will be half starved.

JOAN: Yes, and I expect Blake and the others will want a snack when they get back. Open the door, Tony.

The door opens – and closes.

TONY: We'll go upstairs to the library … (*He stops*) Joan – Joan – look! At the end of the corridor!

The tray drops to the ground.

JOAN: (*Softly*) It's … it's Holly!

TONY: Quickly, darling!

FADE DOWN scene.

FADE IN.

JOAN: Is – is he dead?

TONY: No. No, I don't think so. Let's get him on to the settee.

JOAN: He must have fallen down the stairs …

TONY: (*Grimly*) M'm …

JOAN: Darling, you don't think …

TONY: Get some hot water, Joan. And a towel, too. I'm afraid his head looks pretty bad.

JOAN: Yes, all right, darling.

There is a pause.

TONY: (*Suddenly*) Joan … what is it? Joan, darling, what is it? Don't stand there as if …

JOAN: (*Softly*) Tony … look! Through the window – across the lake.

TONY: Across the … (*Suddenly*) It's the mill! Cawtry's Mill … it's on fire!

JOAN: You don't think the Man in the Iron Mask had
           anything to do with …
TONY: (*Desperately*) It must be, Joan! It must be!
JOAN: (*Alarmed*) Tony … where are you going?
TONY: Listen, Joan, I don't know what's happened
           over there at the mill, but this is our chance –
           the chance we've been waiting for.
JOAN: What do you mean?
TONY: I mean simply this, dear. I'm going upstairs.
           I'm going to find out who is in his room – and
           who isn't. Stay with Holly, Joan. If anything
           happens scream – and use this gun.
JOAN: Darling, do be careful. Do be careful!
TONY: (*In the background*) Don't worry, Joan!
A pause.
SERGEANT HOLLY starts to groan.
He is slowly regaining his senses.
HOLLY: What's happening? Where … where am I?
JOAN: It's all right, sergeant. There's nothing to worry
           about.
HOLLY: But I don't understand … Oh! Oh, my head!
Siboku arrives on the scene.
SIBOKU: Miss Dixon!
JOAN: (*Surprised*) Siboku! Oh, what a fright you gave
           me! What is it, Siboku?
SIBOKU: Mill burn … Siboku … not like!
JOAN: (*Puzzled*) Siboku … not like?
SIBOKU: Tuan Angelo … him take Siboku to mill …
           Siboku live in mill many days … many days!
Knocking is heard on the front door.
It is very heavy knocking.
JOAN: That's Blake! Open the door, Siboku. Quickly!!
The door is opened.
BLAKE and TINKER enter.

66

SIBOKU: Tuan Blake!

JOAN: Mr Blake … thank heavens you're back!

BLAKE: Hello, what's happened to Holly?

JOAN: We found him here a few minutes ago, and Tony rushed upstairs.

BLAKE: He looks pretty groggy if I'm any …

His words are cut short by a sudden scream.

It is TONY shouting for help.

TINKER: Crikey, listen! That's Tony!

BLAKE: It came from the library.

JOAN: (*Desperately afraid*) Blake … Tony must have found him … the Man in the Iron Mask.

A second scream is heard which is followed by a heavy thud.

BLAKE: (*Grimly*) Come on, Tinker!

FADE SCENE.

FADE IN of TONY shouting for help.

A small table overturns.

BLAKE and TINKER arrive, obviously rather out of breath.

BLAKE immediately tries the door handle.

BLAKE: It's locked, Tinker!

BLAKE throws himself against the door.

From inside the room can be heard the sound of a tremendous struggle.

TONY is screaming for help.

JOAN: (*Frightened*) Oh, do be quick! Oh, do …

BLAKE: (*Desperately*) We've got to get this door open – Tinker!

TINKER: Here, let me give you a hand, guv'nor!

Both TINKER and BLAKE throw their weight against the door.

From inside the room TONY continues his death struggle with the MAN IN THE IRON MASK.

BLAKE: My God, Tinker, we've got to be quick if we're going to save Tony!

They continue to throw their weight against the heavy door.

TINKER: (*Exhausted*) We'll never break this door, guv'nor … not like this!

BLAKE: No. No, I'm afraid not.

TONY gives a last desperate scream for help.

It is followed by the wild insane laughter of the MAN IN THE IRON MASK.

TINKER: Guv'nor … we've got to do something.

BLAKE: (*Desperately*) Stand back, Tinker!

BLAKE throws his weight against the door in a final desperate attempt.

The door gives in slightly and there is the sudden splintering of a panel.

TINKER: You've done it!! You've done it!!

JOAN: Be quick! Oh, for God's sake be quick, Mr Blake!

BLAKE and TINKER continue tearing the panel out of the door.

TINKER: It's all right, I can open it now, guv'nor!

The door is thrown open.

JOAN: Tony!! (*Screaming*) Tony!! Mr Blake, he's – he's – dead!

TINKER: The swine's disappeared! He must 'ave known about the secret passage an' done a bunk as soon …

JOAN: (*Crying*) Tony! Tony!!

BLAKE: Miss Dixon, please! Let me have a look at him.

TINKER: (*Excitedly*) Look 'ere, guv'nor, if we're going to follow this bloke then …

BLAKE: No! There's still a chance I may be able to bring Tony round if I work fast. Get that cushion, Tinker. Quickly! Put it under his head.

JOAN: (*Sobbing*) Is – is there a chance?

BLAKE: Artificial respiration may do the trick … it's difficult to say.

BLAKE is working furiously on TONY in an attempt to revive him.

There is a pause.

JOAN is sobbing.

TINKER: Let me have a shot, guv'nor!

BLAKE: (*Slightly exhausted*) No. I want you to check up on the rest of the people here. Quick, Tinker!

TINKER: O.K., guv'nor!

TINKER departs.

JOAN: Oh, you must save him, Mr Blake! You must!!

BLAKE: It – it takes time, Miss Dixon. Please be patient!

SIBOKU: (*Quietly*) Tuan Blake strong man. Work very hard.

BLAKE: Oh, hello, Siboku … so you've arrived, eh?

A slight pause.

The door is suddenly thrown open and BENITO enters.

JOAN: (*Amazed*) Benito!!

BENITO: What – what on earth has been going on here? (*Alarmed*) Why – Tony!

JOAN: Benito, please be quiet! Tony's had a very bad … (*She suddenly stops*)

BENITO: What's the matter? What are you looking at?

JOAN: (*Puzzled*) You've cut your head, Benito. It looks as if you might … almost … have been … in a fight.

BENITO: Yes, I fell … down the steps into the kitchen and …

BLAKE: Into the kitchen?

BENITO: Yes. There's rather a lot of steps … thirteen, I believe.

BLAKE: Thirteen? An unlucky number … thirteen, Mr Benito Marthioly. (*As an afterthought*) So I'm told.

FADE IN closing music.

END OF EPISODE FOUR

EPISODE FIVE

PRELUDE
TO MURDER

OPEN TO:

ANNOUNCER: At the end of episode four, Tony had been attacked by the Man in the Iron Mask and left for dead while Benito Marthioly came on to the scene.

FADE IN of music.

FADE DOWN of music.
FADE IN of JOAN DIXON.

JOAN: (*Puzzled*) You've cut your head, Benito. It looks as if you might … almost … have been … in a fight.

BENITO: Yes, I fell … down the steps into the kitchen and …

BLAKE: Into the kitchen?

BENITO: Yes. There's rather a lot of steps … thirteen, I believe.

BLAKE: Thirteen? An unlucky number … thirteen, Mr Benito Marthioly.

BENITO: What do you mean? What do you mean by that?

JOAN: (*Suddenly*) Oh, do be quiet, Benito! (*Anxiously*) Mr Blake, is Tony going to be all right, or …

BLAKE: He's had a pretty near squeak, Miss Dixon … but I think he'll pull through all right … (*With a sigh of relief*) He's breathing better …

BENITO: (*Dazed*) I can't understand it. I thought that Tony was behind all this … this dreadful business, and yet … (*Suddenly*) My God, what a fool I've been … I see it all now … I see it all …

BLAKE: Just <u>what</u> do you see, Mr Marthioly?

BENITO: Why … Angus, of course! Angus must be …
            the Man in the Iron Mask.

*At this moment the noise of the heavy door knocker is heard
from the main lounge.*

BLAKE: That's the Inspector! Would one of you be
            good enough to …

JOAN: Of course, I'll go.

BENITO: It's all right, Joan. I'll see to it.

BENITO leaves the library.

A slight pause.

BLAKE continues to work on TONY CARRADINE.

JOAN: (*Anxiously*) Mr Blake, Tony's going to be all
            right, isn't he?

BLAKE: Yes – yes, I think so.

BLAKE straightens himself and utters a sigh of relief.

BLAKE: Ah … that's better! (*A tiny pause*) Now, Miss
            Dixon, I'd rather like to hear about what
            happened after we left the Castle.

JOAN: Well, when you and Tinker and Inspector
            MacTaggart went off to explore, Tony and I
            went into the kitchen. We intended to make
            some coffee for Uncle Peter and the others.
            You see, they were all in separate rooms so
            naturally they couldn't …

BLAKE: I understand.

JOAN: We made the coffee and started off on our
            rounds. The first person we came across,
            however, was Holly. He was at the foot of the
            stairs, and looked in a pretty bad condition. We
            carried him on to the settee in the lounge, and
            then I noticed the mill burning. You can see it
            from the main window. When Tony saw it he
            dashed upstairs to discover who was missing.
            Well, the rest you know …

BLAKE:	M'm …
JOAN:	(*Almost desperately*) Mr Blake … do you think we'll ever find out who this dreadful person is? This evil … wicked …
BLAKE:	(*Softly*) We shall find out, Miss Dixon. We shall find out …
JOAN:	But … but it seems so horrible. It might be someone here … Someone we all know, and … and like …
BLAKE:	I am practically certain in my own mind who the murderer is, but proof is impossible without the missing contents of Angelo Marthioly's document box.
JOAN:	But if the murderer got those papers, surely he'd destroy them …
BLAKE:	Not necessarily.

The door opens.

BLAKE:	Ah, here's the Inspector.
MacTAGGART:	Well, this is a pretty kettle of fish, Blake! How's Mr Carradine?
BLAKE:	He's all right now … but it'll be quite a while before he can tell us anything. It was damn near touch and go …
MacTAGGART:	(*Irritated*) T't … t't! I don't know I'm sure … things seem to get worse. Poor old Holly seems in a bad way, too.
BLAKE:	Yes, I'd better have a look at him.

The door opens.
It is Tinker.

TINKER:	'Ello, Inspector!
BLAKE:	(*Briskly*) Well, Tinker?
TINKER:	I checked up on everybody, like you said. Mr Peter Marthioly was in his

75

	room … in bed asleep … Old what's-his-name Angus was in his room reading; but Mr Benito's room was empty. It didn't look to me as if it had even been occupied.
BLAKE:	That's interesting.
MacTAGGART:	It certainly is. Well, Mr Benito?
BENITO:	Talk about making a mountain out of a molehill! I went downstairs … to the kitchen … I was hungry. When I came out of the kitchen, and into the great hall, I saw Holly on the settee.
BLAKE:	And then what happened?
BENITO:	Why … I came straight up here …
MacTAGGART:	How was it you didn't see Holly on your way down to the kitchen?
BENITO:	(*Irritated*) Because I went down by the back stairs …
MacTAGGART:	M'm – a pity.
BENITO:	For once I'm inclined to agree with you, Inspector, I fell down most of them.
JOAN:	Mr Blake, do you think we might take Tony to one of the bedrooms?
BLAKE:	Yes. Yes, I don't see why not. MacTaggart, will you and Siboku carry him to the bedroom at the head of the main stairs? (*Suddenly looking round*) Siboku! Where have … Oh, there you are!
SIBOKU:	Siboku very happy to help police inspector.
MacTAGGART:	M'm …
BLAKE:	And Tinker, will you kindly bring Angus and Peter Marthioly to the library? I

	want to have a chat with them after I've seen Holly.
BENITO:	Shall you want me here as well … in the library, I mean?
BLAKE:	If you please, Mr Benito.
MacTAGGART:	M'm, sounds like a family party. Ought to be jolly.
BLAKE:	You never can tell, Inspector. You never can tell. (*He chuckles*)

FADE SCENE.

FADE IN of several voices.
Suddenly SEXTON BLAKE is heard.

BLAKE:	Thank you, gentlemen! Thank you! Because you have all told your stories very clearly, and I'm most grateful.
PETER:	Mr Blake, do forgive me if I seem a little impatient. But please tell us quite frankly, do you think there's a chance that you'll catch this fiend who masquerades as the Man in the Iron Mask?
BLAKE:	There is more than a chance, Mr Marthioly. I <u>intend</u> to catch him. Indeed, as far as I am concerned there is only one thing lacking for the completion of my case.
PETER:	Oh? And what's that?
BLAKE:	The thing in question … (*Suddenly changing the tone of his voice*) Oh, Inspector, I wonder would you take Siboku and remain with him in the great hall? You can see the bedrooms from there where Tony and Holly are lying …

77

MacTAGGART:	Aye, of course. We mustn't take any chances. Come along, laddie. Miss Dixon is with Mr Carradine, isn't she?
BLAKE:	Yes. Don't disturb them. Both Tony and Holly need plenty of sleep.
MacTAGGART:	O' course.

The door opens and closes.

PETER:	You were saying, Mr Blake, that only one thing is lacking for the completion of a concrete case ...
BLAKE:	Oh yes. I was referring to the documents which were taken from Angelo Marthioly's deed box.
ANGUS:	Documents! What has the Man in the Iron Mask to do with documents! His curse is upon the ...
BENITO:	Quiet, Angus!
ANGUS:	His curse is upon the House of Marthioly!!
BENITO:	Why, Blake, can't you see this old fool is out of his mind? What further proof do you need of his ...?
PETER:	Silence, Benito! I will not have these sudden outbursts of unseemly conduct. Please remember that this is my house and that, in spite of what has happened, I expect you to behave as ordinary intelligent human beings. As for you, Angus, please remember your position in this household!
ANGUS:	Yes, master.
PETER:	(*Calmly*) You were saying, Mr Blake, that you only needed the contents of the deed box to – er – clinch your case. But

	surely the murderer will have destroyed them by now?
BLAKE:	I don't think so. You see, I believe that the papers were gone from the box before the murder took place. In fact, I believe that the vital documents were never found by the Man in the Iron Mask, and that even now … he doesn't know where they are.
BENITO:	(*Staggered*) What!
TINKER:	Crikey, guv'nor!
BLAKE:	That, at any rate, is my belief.

In the background a clock chimes the hour.

BLAKE:	My word, I never realised it was that late.
BENITO:	I think I'll go to bed, Blake. That is, if you've no objections?
BLAKE:	Of course not.
PETER:	All right, Angus … there's no need for you to stay up any later, either.
ANGUS:	Thank you, master.

The door opens and closes.

BLAKE:	Mr Peter, have you any idea what the papers might be? The ones which were stolen from the deed box?
PETER:	None whatsoever I'm afraid.
BLAKE:	M'm – tell me, how long had Siboku been a servant of your brother's?
PETER:	Oh, a good many years I should say. Angelo was a government agent in North Borneo, you know. And as far as I could gather he trusted Siboku implicitly.
BLAKE:	Yes. Yes, I'd rather got that impression. (*Thoughtfully*) You know, Mr Marthioly,

	it is just possible that your brother may have entrusted those precious documents of his to Siboku …
PETER:	M'm … I'd never thought of that … to Siboku. Yes! Yes, that's quite a theory. (*Thoughtfully*) And not at all a bad one.
BLAKE:	One thing I do know. Once those documents are in our hands, the Man in the Iron Mask will be trapped.
PETER:	Well, I hope you are right, Blake. I sincerely hope you are right. (*Yawning*) Oh … excuse me. Well, I think I'll call it a day. Goodnight, Mr Blake. Goodnight, Tinker …
TINKER:	Goodnight.
BLAKE:	Goodnight.

The door opens and closes.

TINKER:	(*Suddenly*) Well, crikey, guv'nor, you haven't half been chatty. Why, the Man in the Iron Mask might have heard every word. Remember there's probably dozens o' secret passages.
BLAKE:	Ssh! Yes … I was thinking of that, Tinker.
TINKER:	Then all that about Siboku an' the secret documents was just eyewash?
BLAKE:	Perhaps, Tinker … perhaps …
TINKER:	(*Irritated*) But look 'ere, I don't want to be poking my nose where …
BLAKE:	(*Quietly*) It's a bait, Tinker. A bait to catch the murderer. If Siboku <u>has</u> got the documents then our trap is all the more certain.
TINKER:	(*Amazed*) Crikey!

The door opens.

BLAKE:	Hello! Why, Miss Dixon! I hope Tony isn't any worse.
JOAN:	Oh, Mr Blake, please come quickly. He seems terribly restless …
BLAKE:	I'll come at once. (*START FADE*) Tinker, you might trip along to our room and get my medical outfit. You know the case …

FADE SCENE.

FADE IN of INSPECTOR MacTAGGART's voice.

MacTAGGART:	M'm … Well, ye certainly tell a pretty exciting yarn, I'll say that for ye, Siboku.
SIBOKU:	It is true … every word. Tuan Angelo very great man. Siboku always servant of Tuan Angelo.
MacTAGGART:	Yes, well the poor devil is dead now, so …
SIBOKU:	Death does not matter. It is like the falling of leaves in autumn.
MacTAGGART:	M'm … er … m'm …
SIBOKU:	Siboku still serve Tuan Angelo. Siboku still guard the paper … as master commanded.
MacTAGGART:	Yes. Well, when you're a bit older, my lad, you'll … (*Suddenly*) Here, just a minute! What's all this about a paper … what sort of a paper?
SIBOKU:	Paper that Tuan Angelo gave to Siboku … that Siboku guard with life …
MacTAGGART:	Ye gods, man … why did ye no say so before! 'Ere, let me see it quickly … quickly!!!

SIBOKU:	Tuan Angelo says … take care of paper … give to no one.
MacTAGGART:	Listen, Siboku … your master was murdered. That paper will tell us who killed him.
SIBOKU:	Paper … tell … who killed Tuan Angelo?
MacTAGGART:	(*Excitedly*) Yes, Siboku! Yes!!!
SIBOKU:	Then … I show paper. Siboku show paper.

SIBOKU takes a document from beneath the folds of his robes.

SIBOKU:	It's here!
MacTAGGART:	(*Excitedly*) Give it to me, Siboku. Don't worry, I'll … (*Alarmed*) What's that! The – the wall's moving!

Part of the wall moves.

The MAN IN THE IRON MASK appears.

VOICE:	I want those papers. Give them to me.
MacTAGGART:	Who – what are you?
VOICE:	I … want … those … papers …
MacTAGGART:	(*Alarmed*) Don't move, Siboku … he'll shoot!
SIBOKU:	This man … he … kill … Tuan Angelo. This Man in Iron Mask?
MacTAGGART:	(*Desperately*) Don't move, Siboku … he'll shoot.
SIBOKU:	Siboku … not afraid …
VOICE:	Stand back, or I'll shoot!!!
SIBOKU:	Siboku … not afraid …
MacTAGGART:	Don't be a fool, Siboku … For God's sake don't …

The MAN IN THE IRON MASK shoots.

SIBOKU falls – as he does so he utters a faint cry of anguish.

VOICE:	Give me that paper … quickly!
MacTAGGART:	Take it, you swine, and by all that's … (*Suddenly*) Blake!!!
BLAKE:	(*Shouting from background*) There he is, Tinker!!!

A revolver shot is heard followed by the sound of running feet.

FADE DOWN scene.

FADE IN of BLAKE and TINKER with MacTAGGART.

BLAKE:	(*Breathless*) Did you – did you recognise him?
MacTAGGART:	No – he had some sort of a cloak besides the Iron Mask, and …
TINKER:	We've got to get him now, guv'nor … no matter what happens!
BLAKE:	He went up the spiral staircase. He's making for the upper corridor. Come along, Tinker!!

FADE IN of BLAKE, TINKER and INSPECTOR MacTAGGART dashing upstairs.

FADE DOWN scene.

FADE IN.

TINKER:	(*Breathless*) He's disappeared … guv'nor …
MacTAGGART:	(*Exhausted*) Aye, aye … the devil's beat us by the look o' things.
BLAKE:	(*Suddenly excited*) Look! Look!!!
TINKER:	It's that panel, guv'nor! It's just closing!
MacTAGGART:	He's gone down that blasted tunnel again. Quickly, Blake!!

BLAKE:	Get the panel open again, Tinker.
TINKER:	'Ere we are! Here's the blinkin' catch.
MacTAGGART:	Get it open. For gawd's sake get it open!

The heavy stone panel moves away from the wall.

BLAKE:	Quick … inside!!
MacTAGGART:	There's something burning. It's the papers – he's set them on fire.
TINKER:	We'd better get a move on, guv'nor – he's got a start on us, an' unless …
BLAKE:	Yes. Come on, MacTaggart! We can deal with the papers later!

We hear the sound of running feet.

MacTAGGART:	There seems to be a devil of a lot of bats down here. Brr!!!
TINKER:	Yes. I felt one or two myself. Reckon they must have been asleep judging by …
BLAKE:	Yes.

BLAKE stops running.

BLAKE:	Yes … the bats – we disturbed them. Fools!
MacTAGGART:	What is it, Blake? What's the matter?
BLAKE:	The bats … don't you see? They flapped out at us as we passed. They were asleep, and …
MacTAGGART:	(*Bewildered*) Well?
BLAKE:	… and we disturbed them. That means nobody else has been this way.
MacTAGGART:	But … the Man in the Iron Mask?
BLAKE:	He never came this way. He just opened the secret panel and threw the burning papers inside. It was a decoy and we fell for it.
MacTAGGART:	Well, I'll …

BLAKE:	And now that devil's prowling about the place and we're down here in this passage.
MacTAGGART:	My God, Blake …
TINKER:	Yes, an' once he finds Tony and Joan, why –
BLAKE:	(*Desperately*) Come on, back to the entrance as fast as you can. Quickly! Quickly!!

We hear the sound of running feet etc.
FADE SCENE.

FADE IN of JOAN DIXON's voice.

JOAN:	(*Quietly*) Now don't worry – don't worry, darling. Just lie back and rest.
TONY:	(*Dazed*) I … I can't remember anything, Joan. It's … it's almost … Oh, my head!
JOAN:	Now don't talk, darling. You'll feel much better when you've had a sleep.
TONY:	Don't … Don 't leave me, Joan … I …
JOAN:	It's all right, darling. Now don't worry, it's all right.
TONY:	(*Bewildered*) He … he attacked me, Joan … I was so surprised. And that mask … staring at me like a … a …
JOAN:	Quiet, darling. Now go to sleep, Tony … that's better, my sweet.
TONY:	There's … there's someone at the door … Listen!
JOAN:	No, it's nothing, Tony. Now do go to sleep, darling!
TONY:	(*With a sigh*) Oh … I feel … so tired.

A pause.
The door opens.

JOAN: (*Suddenly*) Who is it? (*Alarmed*) Who's there? (*Desperately frightened*) Oh! (*Terrified*) Tony! Tony!!

It is – the MAN IN THE IRON MASK.

TONY: (*Weakly, almost asleep*) What – what is it, Joan?

JOAN: It's – it's the Man in the Iron Mask! (*She utters a terrific shriek for help*)

The MAN IN THE IRON MASK laughs.

He is greatly amused, but his laugh is cold and inhuman.

FADE IN of closing music.

END OF EPISODE FIVE

EPISODE SIX

THE CASE IS CLOSED

OPEN TO:

ANNOUNCER: At the end of episode five, Joan was looking after Tony who was lying seriously ill after being attacked by the Man in the Iron Mask. Blake, Tinker and MacTaggart had been lured away by a ruse. Suddenly, in a lonely room where Joan is sitting, appears the Man in the Iron Mask. Listen now to what follows.

FADE IN of music.

FADE DOWN music.

FADE IN of JOAN DIXON speaking to TONY CARRADINE.

JOAN: Quiet, darling. Now go to sleep, Tony … that's better, my sweet.

TONY: There's … there's someone at the door … Listen!

JOAN: No, it's nothing, Tony. Now do go to sleep, darling!

TONY: (*With a sigh*) Oh … I feel … so tired.

A pause.

The door opens.

JOAN: (*Suddenly*) Who is it? (*Alarmed*) Who's there? (*Desperately frightened*) Oh! (*Terrified*) Tony! Tony!!

It is – the MAN IN THE IRON MASK.

TONY: (*Weakly, almost asleep*) What – what is it, Joan?

JOAN: It's – it's the Man in the Iron Mask! (*She utters a terrific shriek for help*)

The MAN IN THE IRON MASK laughs.

He is greatly amused, but his laugh is cold and inhuman.

VOICE: Stand away from the bed …

JOAN: What – what do you want?

VOICE: Tony Carradine ... must die ...

JOAN: (*Desperately*) No! No!

VOICE: He knows my identity ... for that ... he must die!

JOAN: No! No!

TONY: (*Weakly*) Joan ... what is it? What's the matter?

JOAN: (*Suddenly shouting for help*) Blake! Blake! Blake!!

VOICE: (*Amused*) It's no use shouting for Sexton Blake. I've taken care of him all right. (*He chuckles*)

JOAN: You're lying! You're lying!

VOICE: I don't think so, my dear. I don't think so ...

JOAN: (*Almost sobbing*) What ... what are you going to do?

VOICE: On the other side of the lake I have a car waiting for me. If you come with me ... Carradine shall live.

JOAN: But – but that's impossible! Besides, what good will that do?

VOICE: It will give me security. You will remain my prisoner for so long as the law leaves me alone. Once let them interfere and – (*He chuckles softly to himself*)

JOAN: (*Terrified*) No! No!!

TONY: (*Obviously exhausted*) Don't go, Joan! Don't go!

VOICE: Is that your answer?

JOAN: No! No – I'll come, but ... please leave Tony – alone!

VOICE: (*Suddenly rather desperate*) Then hurry ... I have no time to waste ...

TONY: (*Desperately*) Don't leave me, Joan!
                 Don't leave me … don't leave me …
VOICE: Hurry!
JOAN: (*Sobbing*) I'm … I'm coming …
TONY: (*Frantic and very weak*) Joan! Joan!
                 Don't go, Joan! Joan! (*He commences to
                 sob*)

FADE SCENE.

FADE IN of SEXTON BLAKE.

*TINKER and INSPECTOR MacTAGGART are throwing
their weight against the stone panel.*

BLAKE: You were right, MacTaggart. Our only
                 way out of here is to find the hidden
                 switch.
MacTAGGART: (*Breathless*) We'll never force this panel
                 – not if we try till Doomsday. It's no use,
                 Tinker! Take it easy, boy!
TINKER: We've got to get out of 'ere, guv'nor!
                 Don't you realise what that fiend …?
BLAKE: Yes, Tinker. I realise only too well what
                 might be happening. (*Suddenly*) You
                 know, I feel quite sure that one of these
                 stone rosettes is the secret switch, if only
                 we knew which one!
MacTAGGART: There's hundreds of 'em, Blake. We'd
                 never be able to find the right one, not if
                 …
BLAKE: Nevertheless it's our only chance! You
                 start at the other end, Tinker. Pull 'em!
                 Push 'em! Twist 'em … do anything …
                 only find out which one makes the stone
                 move. I'll start at this end and
                 MacTaggart can … (*He stops*)

91

MacTAGGART: (*Anxiously*) What is it, Blake?

BLAKE: I've found it!! Stand back – away from the panel, Tinker!

The stone panel slowly opens.

MacTAGGART: (*Excited*) Ye've done it, Blake! Ye've done it!!!

BLAKE: (*Excitedly*) Come on! We've got to find Tony Carradine.

FADE SCENE.

A door opens.

TINKER: Tony!

MacTAGGART: What are ye doing on the floor, lad, why …

BLAKE: He's exhausted. Get him back on to the bed!

TONY: (*Softly*) Joan … Joan!!

MacTAGGART: He's had some sort of a shock, Blake. He's much worse.

BLAKE: Yes. (*Quietly*) Tony, listen … this is Blake … Blake … Sexton Blake …

TONY: (*Almost in a coma*) Joan … don't leave me … don't leave me …

BLAKE: Tony, listen. This is your friend … Blake … Sexton Blake …

TONY: Sexton … Blake? (*Suddenly*) You've got to find Joan. He's taken Joan away … away …

BLAKE: (*Desperately*) Listen, Tony. Try and pull yourself together.

MacTAGGART: For God's sake, laddie, get a grip on yerself!

TONY: The Man in the Iron Mask took … Joan away … he had a car on the other side …

	on the other side of the lake, and … and …
MacTAGGART:	My God, do ye hear that, Blake!!
TINKER:	(*Alarmed*) Guv'nor!
BLAKE:	Quick, Tinker! The aeroplane!

FADE SCENE.

FADE IN of SEXTON BLAKE shouting.
They are outside the castle.

BLAKE:	Get that ballast off her floats, Mac! Into the cabin, Tinker.
MacTAGGART:	How many can this thing take?
BLAKE:	Only two. You'll have to stay behind, Inspector. (*Shouting*) Contact!

The aeroplane starts.

TINKER:	(*Shouting from the background*) O.K., guv'nor … jump in.
MacTAGGART:	(*Excitedly*) Before ye go, Blake – who <u>is</u> the Man in the Iron Mask?
BLAKE:	Count your suspects. See who's missing at the castle … (*Shouting*) See you later!!

The aeroplane roars.
FADE UP of the aeroplane engine.

FADE DOWN as the plane steadies itself.

TINKER:	Good job there's a decent moon.
BLAKE:	Yes. (*Quietly*) We'd better fly fairly low to start with.
TINKER:	(*After a pause*) There's a shed over on the right. Look!
BLAKE:	M'm … That's probably where he kept the car.
TINKER:	That's not a main road is it, guv'nor?

93

BLAKE: No. I shouldn't think so. Looks too bumpy. (*Pause*) We'll probably spot him over the brow of the hill.

TINKER: Yes. (*A slight pause*) You know it beats me why the swine should want to take Miss Dixon, surely …

BLAKE: I suppose he's got some crazy notion about holding her as … as … a sort of hostage. It's the kind of thing a crazy devil like … (*Suddenly*) Hello, there's a wood over on the right. That's lucky.

TINKER: He may have switched his headlights off.

BLAKE: Yes, keep your eyes skinned, Tinker. (*A pause*) I suppose he's driving Tony's old Bentley … he didn't keep a car himself.

TINKER: Who didn't, guv'nor?

BLAKE: The Man in the Iron Mask, Tinker.

TINKER: But – but who is he?

BLAKE: One of three people. Peter Marthioly … Angus … or Benito. One of those three, Tinker, killed Angelo Marthioly for the possession of a certain document. The same person attacked you, Tony, Siboku, Sergeant Holly, MacTaggart and myself because we intended, at all cost, to bring him to justice. He also attacked Peter Marthioly, for a less obvious, though equally finite reason. Correlate those facts, Tinker, and there is only one person who can be … the Man in the Iron Mask!

TINKER: M'm …

BLAKE: (*After a pause*) We should have spotted him by now.

TINKER: Yes. The wood is beginning to thin out a bit.

BLAKE: I'm turning back. If he once gives us the slip it's going to be awkward.

TINKER: There's a lot of thick trees about two hundred …

BLAKE: (*Suddenly*) There he goes!!

TINKER: Blimey, he's shifting!

BLAKE: He's aiming for the new road – it's over on the other side.

TINKER: We're getting lower.

BLAKE: It's all right. Hold on, Tinker!

TINKER: I don't see how we can stop him, guv'nor! Not with Miss Dixon in the car.

BLAKE: No, they mustn't crash. (*Thoughtfully*) There's just one chance. Here, you take the controls! Keep her at about this speed … don't get ahead of the car if you can help it.

TINKER: (*Alarmed*) What are you going to do?

BLAKE: I'm going to drop on to the car.

TINKER: Guv'nor … you can't do that – it's suicide!

BLAKE: It's all right, Tinker. I know what I'm doing. The road runs straight for about two or three miles. I'm going out on to the floats now – keep her steady.

TINKER: O.K.

BLAKE: If you have to land don't forget to run your wheels down.

TINKER: Watch yourself, guv'nor!

There is a sudden rush of cold air and the roar of the engine.

BLAKE: (*Shouting*) Down, Tinker! Down!!

FADE IN of the motor car travelling at a very fast speed.

There is the roar of the aeroplane as it passes overhead.

SEXTON BLAKE jumps.

He lands in the car.

JOAN gives a sudden exclamation.

JOAN: Sexton Blake!

BLAKE: Stop this car! Stop this car, or I'll shoot!

VOICE: Shoot! Shoot, curse you … and be damned!!

BLAKE: (*Desperately*) Stop this car!!

JOAN: Look out!! We're going for the trees!

BLAKE: (*Desperately*) For God's sake, man, don't. Get down, Joan! Keep down!

The car hits the trees with a resounding thud.

There is the sudden smashing of glass.

The car starts to burn.

FADE SCENE.

FADE UP of TINKER.

He is out of breath through running.

TINKER: Guv'nor! Guv'nor, are you all right?

BLAKE: Yes … yes, I'm only … a bit shaken that's all. (*Suddenly*) Where's Joan? My God, we must get her out of this awful …

TINKER: She's over there on the bank, guv'nor. She was thrown clear of the car so I think she's o.k.

BLAKE: Oh, good! (*Shouting*) Joan! Joan, are you all right?

JOAN: (*From the background*) Yes … yes … I'm all right … don't bother about me!

BLAKE: The man we want is under the car, Tinker, we'd better work fast if …

TINKER: Yes, there's an awful smell of petrol. She might go up if we're not – It's all right, guv'nor, I can get through there.

BLAKE: If you can, Tinker, I think we may be able to get him out.

Part of the wreckage is moved.

BLAKE: Watch yourself!

A slight pause.

TINKER: I've got him. Can – can – you get hold of – of his shoulders?

BLAKE: (*Bending over the wreckage*) Yes … (*Slight pause*) He looks pretty bad.

TINKER: It's difficult to tell with this blinkin' cloak on. We'd better get the mask off, too.

BLAKE: Let's get him clear of the car first. You take his feet, Tinker.

TINKER: O.K.

BLAKE: We'll carry him over to where Miss Dixon is. Steady, Tinker!

FADE SCENE.

FADE UP.

JOAN: Mr Blake … is he dead?

BLAKE: No. No, I don't think so. But he's very badly hurt.

There is a tiny pause.

JOAN: Who is he? Who is … the Man in the Iron Mask?

BLAKE: You'll get rather a shock, Joan … I'm afraid. You see … you were rather fond of him. (*A tiny pause*) Tinker … take off the iron mask.

TINKER: How does it go – is there …?

BLAKE: There's a catch on the side. Wait a second, let me lift him …

TINKER: That's better. I've got it!

The mask is taken off the face of PETER MARTHIOLY.

JOAN: Uncle … Peter!!!

BLAKE: Yes, I'm afraid so, Miss Dixon. Peter Marthioly.

FADE IN of music.

FADE music down slowly.
FADE IN of chatter and the clinking of wine glasses.

ANGUS: Another glass of wine, Mr Tony?

TONY: No thank you, Angus.

BENITO: (*Laughing*) We mustn't get the bridegroom drunk, Angus!

ANGUS: (*Amused*) No, Mr Benito … indeed not …

JOAN: I'm so glad you were able to get here for the reception, Mr Blake. Somehow, after all you've done for us, it wouldn't have seemed – just right – without you. (*Laughing*) And, of course, Tinker!

BLAKE: That's very nice of you to say so, Joan.

TONY: You know, there's just one thing about all this business, Blake, I don't quite understand.

BLAKE: Oh! And what's that?

TONY: Well, why <u>did</u> Uncle Peter murder my uncle – surely …

BLAKE: Because he was afraid of losing his wealth and position. You see, being the eldest son. And since there was apparently no will, Peter inherited the estates of Marthioly. But Angelo discovered a will … a will which was in his favour. Peter realised this and murdered his brother to stop him claiming his heritage.

JOAN commences to cry.

JOAN: How … dreadful …

TONY: Don't cry, darling … not today … (*After a slight pause*) Blake, promise me that you will put the iron mask beyond the reach of … mortal men. Promise me!

BLAKE: (*Quietly*) The bottom of the sea shall be its last resting place, Tony. I promise.

Suddenly BENITO starts knocking on the table.

98

JOAN: Sh! Benito is going to make a speech.

TINKER: I was afraid of that.

There is a slight pause.

BENITO: (*Clearing his throat*) Joan … Tony … and my dear friends. I am going to ask you to drink a toast. A toast to the man who came here – to the Castle of Saint Marguerite … many days ago. A man, for whose bravery and inspired courage we shall always be grateful. Sexton Blake!

TONY: Sexton Blake!

JOAN: Sexton Blake!

ANGUS: Sexton Blake!

TINKER: Sexton Blake!

BENITO: Sexton Blake!

The glasses fall one by one into the fireplace.

FADE IN of closing music.

THE END